TRACKER

**Center Point
Large Print**

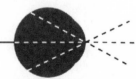

**This Large Print Book carries the
Seal of Approval of N.A.V.H.**

TRACKER

William Vance

CENTER POINT PUBLISHING
THORNDIKE, MAINE

This Center Point Large Print edition
is published in the year 2011 by arrangement with
Golden West Literary Agency.

First US edition: Avalon Books.
First UK edition: Gunsmoke.

The text of this Large Print edition is unabridged.
In other aspects, this book may vary
from the original edition.
Printed in the United States of America
on permanent paper.
Set in 16-point Times New Roman type.

ISBN: 978-1-61173-247-4

Library of Congress Cataloging-in-Publication Data

Vance, William E.
Tracker / William Vance. — Center Point large print ed.
p. cm.
ISBN 978-1-61173-247-4 (library binding : alk. paper)
1. Large type books. I. Title.
PS3572.A425T73 2011
813′.54—dc22

2011030020

TRACKER

CHAPTER 1

The renegades, though out of sight, followed him as he followed his thief. They would hang on until they caught him or he rode out of their hell.

The blazing sun threw vindictive rays down upon the land, raising a shimmering curtain of heat even in late afternoon. Beneath the horse's hoofs the earth was sandy, and seldom saw rain to bring new life to the land.

The landscape was littered with cactus and mesquite, the former appearing almost human in distant perspective. More than once Sam Tracker had stiffened in the saddle at a manlike figure, then relaxed as it resolved itself into cactus. Now, he removed his hat, even as the stocky horse under him cantered heavily through the sand. He used his neckerchief, wet with sweat, to mop more sweat from his forehead, thinking, *I'll catch up before nightfall.* He felt a savage exultation rise in him and it made the misery of desert travel tolerable.

The pounding horse beneath his knees faltered when the shot blasted the stillness. Tracker jerked the reins with one hand and his other went to his gun, as the gelding stumbled, falling. The second shot brought a burn of flame at his bottom rib. The horse tucked under and Tracker rolled out of the saddle. His momentum flung him through the sand

and he skidded into a cluster of hot brown rocks. He shook the sand out of his pistol as he looked for movement in the furnacelike land ahead.

Nothing stirred in the hot stillness except the shimmer of heat waves.

A vinegaroon scuttled across the sand, its stinger tail raised high. Tracker lifted his boot and dropped it atop the insect, hearing its crusty shell crunch. The scorpionlike insect remained imbedded on his spur and he used the barrel of his Colt to scrape it off.

Squinting from under the brim of his big black hat, he saw nothing—only the trail he'd followed for six days, the trail which disappeared over a sandy rise ahead.

"Now how in hell," he asked aloud, "did I ride into that one?"

It was plain to him even as he asked the question. He'd gotten close enough to raise an eagerness that wouldn't be denied. *A man can hurry himself to death,* he thought grimly. A lean man, of rawhide and whipcord, a tobacco brown face and unjudging gray eyes, Sam Tracker glanced briefly at the front of his shirt, saw the red of blood, felt the burn of gunshot, and cursed softly. He looked at the black gelding, still down. The horse returned his look with patient brown eyes. The white of bone projected from the front leg. The horse whinnied and tried to rise, sinking back as the leg flapped uselessly.

Tracker turned again and surveyed the country. It was like the country he'd been riding through—shallow, sandy arroyos, layer on layer, rising to the distant purple haze of mountains. A movement caught his eye. Ahead of him, far ahead, dust lifted from the band of horses he'd been chasing.

Tracker swore softly and watched them out of sight and it was as though the trail had ended. The man who'd robbed him, taken his woman, and then tried to kill him, rode on with the finest bunch of horses he'd ever seen.

He rose and walked over to the horse with the broken leg. He knelt beside the animal, rubbing its neck as it nickered softly, as though calling for help. Then he put the muzzle of the Colt against the head, thumbed back the hammer, squeezed off a shot that seemed to pierce his own heart. The gelding dropped its head, stiffened, and relaxed with finality.

Looking toward the faint dust cloud, Tracker said aloud, "There's another score to settle, friend."

He squatted beside the horse, unbuckled the girth and bellyband, and worried the saddle loose. He dragged it aside, stripped the bridle from the gelding and tossed it on the saddle. Then he pulled his shirt out of his pants and rolled it under his arms, his chin digging his chest as he looked at the raw red furrow around his ribs. The blood still oozed from it.

He slipped the neckerchief over his head, damped it from his canteen, and sponged the wound. The pain was still there but it wasn't bad, he reflected. He opened his bedroll, cut a strip from his blanket, and awkwardly wrapped it around the furrowed flesh, tucking in the end. This done he stuffed his shirt back in his pants, glanced at the westering sun, shouldered his saddle and walked on.

Seven days ago he was engaged in successful negotiations with Army procurement officers in Prescott about horses he hoped the Army would eventually adopt. The Army was receptive to the idea; so impressed in fact, they signed a contract equipping one troop with the animals that had been bred for stamina and speed, a cross between a tough cow horse and pure Arabian.

Returning to his ranch, Tracker found it cleaned out by his partner, Kirby Landers. Sam Tracker, being the kind of man he was, stopped only long enough to write the Army telling them there'd be a delay in fulfilling the contract.

He meant to deliver to the Army but first he had to find Landers—and his horses.

Coming up a rise, he was met by a hot blast of wind that was fanning out of the southwest. Sand rattled against his boots, rising to his hips as the wind stiffened; then sand and dust was filling the air, hot and suffocating. His eyes stung. His throat clogged. He pushed the neckerchief, dry now, up over his nose and pushed on stubbornly.

The trail was brushed out by the wind before he traveled a quarter mile. He threw the saddle down in the lee of a giant cactus and lowered himself to the ground. He found a measure of relief there. The sun, screened by blowing dust and sand, seemed to flee behind the mountain. Darkness came down quickly. He slept for a time.

Tracker came awake as suddenly as he dropped off. He lay there quietly, seeing a flicker on the horizon. At first he thought it a flash of heat lightning. The wind had died. Stars seemed to hang just overhead. The flash he'd seen blossomed into a fire in the distance.

He raised to his knees, stretched, and then stood upright. Sam Tracker was a tall, quiet man with a lot of living behind him. He talked little and listened much. He had the knack of driving to the heart of a problem immediately. He was impatient with indirectness. He stood there now, staring out into the darkness at the flickering light of fire. He knew almost at once that his stalkers, the Apache renegades, had found his horse. He felt a savage surge of anger at the thought of them squatting around the gelding, cutting off chunks of meat. They would stay there until they ate the horse.

Or would they?

In the past three days he'd caught one glimpse of them as they trailed him. Four, perhaps five, all unmounted, reservation breakaways. They wanted weapons and horses, and he was fair game for them. They might have sent half their number on, but he didn't think so. After feasting on his horse they'd come after him, intent on taking his weapons.

They don't like that wind any better than I, he thought. He decided that they'd eat the horse and then stalk him.

He yanked the Winchester saddle gun from the boot and levered a shell into the chamber. He held it in the crook of his arm while he put another shell in the chamber he normally carried empty under the hammer of his Colt .45; then he started walking directly toward the fire.

Out of Mississippi by way of Texas, Sam Tracker was part and parcel of the Civil War, even though it was over before his birth. He was born of parents who were not slaveholders, the poor whites of the back country. Sam's father had migrated to Texas, and out there on the wide sweep of Comanche Country, his father and mother fell to a raiding party. At seventeen, Sam became a wanderer until he came on the place near Flagstaff, Arizona, owned by an Eastern tubercular in the last stages of the disease. Sam stayed on, taking care of Jim Strogan, and after his death inheriting the place which Strogan had never named. It became the T-Bar the day after he buried Jim Strogan on the hill above the three-room cabin; the week after that, he bought the

Arab stallion and four years had passed while he'd never sold a horse.

In the four years at the ranch in the valley, surrounded by fir-clad hills, Tracker had increased the herd, breeding fine horses. He had established contact with the Army. Purchasing officers, quartermasters, farriers, and cavalry officers were frequent visitors at the T-Bar. As part of a horse-riding Army, they were interested in better mounts. Tracker was breeding a special horse for a special mission and, as with everything else he did, he used all of his energies to further his plans, even to taking in a partner, Kirby Landers.

He stopped on the ridge of a sand dune, knowing that the higher dunes behind him kept him from sky-lining. The fire was plainly visible, a yellow-red eye in the night. Yet there was an inviting appearance to it. It seemed to say, "Come on in and rest, stranger, by the friendly fire." But that was mockery, he knew. He stood there for fifteen minutes, his senses attuning to what lay ahead.

The wind had begun again, but not so fierce now, scarcely dimming the fire. If it had been blowing toward him, he knew he would smell cooking horse flesh. He felt another knot of anger form in his belly.

The wind could rise again, blotting out everything, and screen them from him. Whatever he had to do, he'd better get on with it. He scowled, watching the fire for another moment and then swinging down the dune, his feet soundless in the deep sand. Down in the arroyo he had only the night around him, nothing more. The stars were bright in a velvet sky. The sand rattled against him in the occasionally gusting wind. He reached the bottom of the shallow arroyo and began to climb the opposite side. He slowed as he approached the rim, edging up until he caught a glimpse of the flickering campfire, then dropping to his knees and crawling the remaining distance. He slithered up over the ridge and down, still close to the ground. He felt an insect scrabble across his hand and hastily flipped it away. He squatted there for a moment, listening.

It was very quiet. There was no sound but the wind moving through the cactus and mesquite, and now and then the rattle of sand against a dried-out plant.

Below the rim he came erect and walked on, the campfire again concealed by the ridge ahead. He crossed another depression and this time he turned down, circling. Wise in the ways of the desert, he knew the Apaches' keen sense of smell could get his scent in the sterile desert air. He slogged around and came upwind at them in a crouch, working his way through the mesquite and cactus that grew higher here.

Wind whispered through the plants. The world was dark, lighted only by the brilliant stars.

Stealthily, he came out between two giant cacti and stood there in the shadows, watching the Apaches squatting around the campfire. They wore breech clouts and leggings that could be pulled up as high as the thigh. One of them had a battered Army hat; the others wore flannel cloths holding their long straight black hair. Two of them wore ragged Army shirts; the other three were naked from the waist up. The braves had built their fire close to the gelding, and they'd had their first fill of horsemeat, the shine of grease around their mouths. They now roasted chunks of flesh, squatting around the fire, each with a piece of meat on mesquite sticks.

That was to take with them along the trail after him, he thought grimly.

He moved out from the cacti and his boot scraped a rock. He could see the five bodies tense as one, and then they exploded back from the fire as the Winchester went up and blasted once, twice. He saw the two men plunge to the ground as he moved back to the cover of the cacti. He couldn't see the other three, but he watched the two motionless men lying just within firelight. He waited without movement, listening to the low whisper of the wind; there was no other sound. A vagrant finger tugged at Tracker's hat.

The shot was a red flash in the night and Tracker fired the rifle at the flash, moving away as he did so and levering in another shell.

Silence again and wind. It was dark but he'd avoided looking directly at the fire and he could see almost as well as at sundown. He had the advantage because, squatting there at the fire, the Apaches would have lost their night vision; but not for long.

He waited, feeling sure that he'd knocked another man down. There was something about hitting a target. You could almost feel it in the gun itself. And that's how it felt. But what about the other two?

The minutes dragged on and Sam Tracker waited, squatting down a mere half dozen paces from where he last shot. Then the two of them came with a rush and a yell; the Winchester blasted again and one tumbled, but the other came on and there was no time to shoot. He caught the knife hand, hanging on to it and at the same time throwing his weight on the Apache, wrapping his legs around the chunky legs. His weight caused them to fall to the ground, with Tracker on top; but only for a moment. The slippery-skinned Apache was out from under and on him, trying for a mortal blow with the knife. Tracker hung grimly on to the knife and brought his knee up into the Apache's crotch, bringing a grunt and lifting him free. The knife hand slackened for a moment and Tracker turned it inward and put all his strength into the savage push. It went home and blood, warm and alive, gushed out on him. The apache fell back and away from him with a gurgling sound that trailed into nothing and his hide-covered feet beat a minute tattoo in the sand.

The wind blew lightly through the cactus and he smelled burning meat. He searched around, found the Winchester and reloaded it. He walked in to the fire. He squatted there and pulled the burning meat from the fire. He rose and kicked sand over the fire. When he couldn't see a trace of red he turned and began walking back to where he had left his saddle.

Miraculously, he found the saddle. He got jerky from the saddle bags and chewed on it, taking a sip of water from the canteen now and then. He was still chewing on the jerky when he fell asleep.

He was up before daybreak and walking again, the heavy saddle bearing down on him. He came down a long, shallow ridge line and saw the dust of a stage in the distance. He shrugged. Not enough money for stage fare to anywhere. Of course they wouldn't turn down a stranded man, but he didn't ask favors of strangers. He kept walking toward the wagon road that became more discernible by the hour. He made it at midday, and later in the afternoon he hitched a ride on a freighter bound for the mines at Quartz Town, north of Mule Creek.

The muleskinner gave him a chance to get settled and then said, "Tough country to be afoot in."

Tracker nodded. "That it is. Funny what difference a horse makes."

"What happened? Step in a hole or somethin'?"

Tracker was silent for a moment and then said, "Sort of like that. What made it rough was a bunch of renegade Apaches trailing me."

"An' they didn't catch you, even you afoot?" the skinner asked incredulously.

Tracker shook his head. "They caught up, all right. Five of them. I left them back there by my horse."

The driver looked sharply at Tracker and saw no brag or boast there. He turned his gaze up toward the sky and saw the circling birds in the far distance. "I wondered about them buzzards," he said musingly. He was silent for a long time and then he said, "Five!"

A quiet man, Sam Tracker kept his own counsel but the driver was hungry for talk. He wanted to know all about it.

"Not much to tell," Tracker said. "When I lost my horse I started walking. After dark I saw the fire and knew the Apaches had found my horse. They'd been walking, too. They stopped long enough to cook some horsemeat. I figured I'd better get them before they got me. I went back and got them."

"Good Lordie," the teamster said.

"How far you going?"

"Up Quartz Town way."

"What's there?"

"Not a town, by dingies. The silver mines. Just the mines, a stamp mill and a bunkhouse for the crew. Yeah, and a company store. That's it."

"Where's the nearest town?"

"Mule Creek. That's about fifteen miles south of Quartz Town. But the road to Quartz Town turns off thirty miles this side Mule Creek."

"Maybe I could ride with you to Quartz Town and then walk on down to Mule Creek."

"I wouldn't recommend it. Purt' rough country. You get off at the forks and I'll bet you'll catch a ride on into Mule." He leaned out to the lee side and spat a stream of brown tobacco juice. "Felipe Ortiz got a shack there at the forks. His ol' lady is purt' good about fixin' a snack for a hungry man."

"I could use one."

"Whyn't you eat a piece o' that horsemeat?"

Tracker frowned. "Be like eating a man," he said bluntly. "For me, anyhow."

"You a wrangler?"

"I got my own spread out of Flagstaff. Raise Army horses."

"Man, they use a sight o' 'em," the driver said. "You figgerin' to sell some horses to the Army at Mule Creek?"

"I didn't know there was any Army at Mule Creek."

"Got a remount station there. An' always lookin' for horses. The right kind, that is. They don't want

19

no bangtails." The driver looked at Tracker and added, "You look kind of beat up. Want to stretch out on the load and catch some shuteye?"

"No, I'll sit, thanks."

"You keep lookin' ahead," the driver said. "Maybe you're follerin' somebody?"

"You got good eyes," Tracker said dryly.

CHAPTER 2

Thirty miles from Mule Creek another dirt road branched off from the main road. The big freight wagon with its six-team span stopped. The driver said, "I turn off here like I told you."

Tracker reached for his saddle, feeling the heat of it as he hefted it to a muscular shoulder. "I sure do thank you," he said, and jumped down, using the broad-rimmed wheel as a step.

The weight of the saddle jarred his side, and he felt perspiration burn into the ragged bullet track rimming his rib.

"Glad to give you a lift, Tracker," the teamster said and his long blacksnake curled out over the mules with a pistol sharp crack. "Get along you long-eared mangy critters!" He grinned down at Sam Tracker. "Don't know why you're headin' for Mule Creek but be careful over there. Town's full o' tinhorns and shysters."

Tracker waved his hand and stood there in the beating down sun, watching the creaking freight wagon move down the road, trailing a thin film of dust that lifted to be whisked away by the wind. The tawny land was empty except for the shimmering heat waves. Back the way he'd come, black dots wheeled and soared in the robin-egg blue sky.

There was an adobe shack in the forks of the

road. A burro stood lethargically in a tiny corral back of the shack. Tracker turned toward the adobe. The teamster had told him he might get food there. His boots scuffed sand as he lugged his saddle over there. Clusters of red chilies hung from the projecting rafters, making a vivid splash of color against the drab brown of the adobe. He dropped his saddle beside the door, fingering the two pieces of silver in his pocket as he rapped with hard knuckles. He'd eaten the last of his jerky the night before, and his belly growled emptily.

A dark-skinned, dark-haired, dark-eyed woman opened the door. She looked at him, and her eyes widened in fright. She said something in Spanish. She said it so fast that Tracker couldn't translate. She started to close the door and hesitated when he pushed his hat back and put out his hand. She was heavy, her breasts full and unsupported, her hips heavy. Her brown legs were plump, her feet bare. Her skin was brown, smooth and unblemished.

He tried to relax the hard-drawn, bitter lines about his mouth. He put a smile on his tobacco-brown face and tried to make it come out his cold gray eyes. He jingled the coins in his pocket and said, in his slow, halting Spanish, "I'm hungry, miss. I'll pay."

She responded with a slow, shy smile and some of the fright left her eyes. There was something reassuring about the big brown man in spite of his watchful eyes. "It's Mrs.," she said shyly. "My husband will be home soon."

"Ah," Tracker said. "I'd never dreamed it. You look so young." It was a lie and he found it difficult. "I'm thirsty, too, Mrs. . . ." He looked at her questioningly.

"Maria Ortiz," she answered. "You wait for my husband, no?" She looked at him anxiously, visibly reassured by what she saw. Tracker's face somehow inspired confidence.

"A thousand thanks," he said, "but I'm late."

She stepped back and he went in, leaving the heat outside the thick adobe walls.

She gave him a drink in a gourd. The interior of the shack was dim and cool and clean. There was a crucifix on the wall, a few sticks of rough homemade furniture. She took the gourd from him and motioned him to the table.

He sat at a clean-scrubbed table, and she brought him beans and tortillas. The beans were cold and the tortillas tough, but he ate hungrily and enjoyed it. She watched him silently.

"Is there much travel on this road?"

"Yes, but in midday, no."

"That makes sense," Tracker said. He followed the glance she laid on him, her eyes widening. Red stained his shirt. He swore mentally. The Apache had spilled a lot of blood on him, and his own blood had stained his shirt.

"Do not be alarmed, Maria," he said hastily. "It's but a slight hurt I suffered when my horse fell."

But she was scared again, and it took all his powers of persuasion to reassure her.

She said, "Come," and he followed her across the room and through a rear door. Leafy vines covered a crude framework built against the adobe shack. A fat brown baby lay sleeping in a rough cradle. She indicated a pallet beside the cradle and motioned for him to lie there.

He stripped off his shirt. The makeshift bandage had slipped down. The raw furrow had begun to scab over. He swabbed at it for a moment with the strip of blanket, but it continued to bleed.

The woman motioned him to lie back on the straw pallet beside the cradle. He lay back, his gun gouging him. He slipped it out of the holster and laid it beside him. He stretched out, relaxing, feeling her soft cool fingers on his skin.

She placed something soothing on his side and bound it. She went into the shack and returned with a brown bottle. She gave him the bottle and tipped her head, motioning him to drink. He tilted the bottle and tasted some strange, bitter potion that made him wrinkle his face.

She smiled at his frown.

"*Gracias, Senora,*" he said. "*Mucho gracias.*"

"You rest here for a time," she said and turned to leave.

"Maria?"

She stopped, turning.

"Did a bunch of horses go through here recently?"

She nodded. "The man let them drink and then went on."

"Which road did he take?"

"The road to Mule Creek, sir."

"Thanks, Maria. Many, many thanks."

She left him and he lay back on the pallet. He felt the bitter medicine he'd drunk in his stomach, warming and soothing, relaxing him. He wanted to get up and go on but he knew it was foolish. He needed to regain some of his strength. He needed to rest. He gave himself up to the weariness of his mind and body. Far away, he thought he heard the jangle of bit chains and the creak of leather but he hadn't the strength nor the power to rouse; he slept.

The thin cry of the baby wakened him. It was dark and a light hot wind stirred the vines. The baby cried fretfully. He sat up, reached for his gun and slipped it back in the holster. He got to his knees and poked a finger at the plump baby. The baby stopped crying and tried to grasp his finger. Tracker rose. He felt better, much better. He heard voices inside the shack and went quietly to the door and listened. He heard a woman's voice, pleading, and then sounds of scuffling feet on the hardpacked dirt floor inside the adobe.

Tracker went through the door and into the

yellow light of the guttering candle lantern. A big man had the Mexican woman in his arms, bending her backward, while she clawed at his face, torrential Spanish pouring from her lips.

Tracker stepped close and jabbed his gun hard into the man's back, bringing a startled grunt from him. "Let her go," he said.

The man stiffened and put his hands up quickly. Maria ran into a corner and turned, her brown face terror-stricken.

The man was huge, with bulky shoulders. His head was too big for even his immense neck, and coarse black hair sprouted above the top of a dirty, collarless shirt that incongruously held a gold collar button. His eyes were like small black olives, and they held a mean but scared look.

"I didn't mean nothin'," he mumbled. "She's jes' a mex."

"I don't mean nothing, either," Tracker said. He moved in quick as a cat, his gun raised. The big man cringed away, trying to cover his head with his arms.

"No, no!" cried Maria.

Tracker stepped back and dropped his gun to his side. "You should be pistol-whipped," he said coldly.

"She—she, oh, hell, man she . . ."

Tracker ignored him, looking at Maria. "He hurt you?"

She came out of the corner, shaking her head.

"Mr. James gives work to my husband some-times," she said.

"That makes it all right for you to wrestle her?"

"Why, sure," James said. "I just stopped to see if ol' Felipe would help me with my horse herd. I'm alluz stoppin' in to pay my respects."

Tracker frowned at James.

"She told me you ain't got a hoss," James said eagerly. "Maybe so you'd like to help me into Mule Creek, if you're goin' that way. I'll pay you ten bucks, too."

At the mention of a horse herd, Tracker's interest deepened. "What have you got?" he asked. He wanted to get to Mule Creek, and this was as quick a way as any. He didn't care for James, but a ride was a ride. And he wanted to look at the horses that James was driving.

"Hosses for Army remount," said James. "Come out and see."

Tracker followed the big sloppy man outside. A string of horses stretched out into the darkness. They were hooked to a light wagon, twenty teams hooked together with rope and iron rings. Tracker struck a match, looked at the brands, and didn't know them. "Suits me," he said.

"Off-wheeler went lame," said James. "I gotta leave 'im here." He took out a big gray about the middle of the string and led the animal back to where Tracker waited. He took out the limping off-wheeler and put in the gray. He took the limping horse to the tiny corral in the rear of the adobe and turned it in with the burro. He came back to where Tracker squatted beside the wagon, already having put his saddle on the gray.

Tracker heard a deep gurgle and the smack of James's lips. The big man passed the bottle to him.

"Better have a snort before we leave," he said. "It's a long ol' ride to Mule Creek."

Tracker took the bottle and had a drink, and then another. The liquor felt raw and burned like liquid fire. He returned the bottle to James wordlessly.

The big man shoved the bottle in his hip pocket. "I'll ride the off-leader," he said. "An' you get on the near-wheeler. Don't let 'em get goin' too fast. We got a heap o' miles to go."

"You said something about ten dollars pay."

The fat man brought out a purse, fished around in the dim light, and brought out two gold pieces. He reluctantly dropped them in Tracker's outstretched hand. "You're a quick one," he chuckled. "Ain't aimin' to pry, but where's your horse?"

"Dead," Tracker said. "Broke his leg. Shot him." He moved toward the shack. "Back in a minute."

"Hurry now, man," James said. "I'm two days late as is."

Tracker gave Maria a five dollar gold piece. Her eyes opened wide and a quick smile came to her face. "Thanks, thanks, may God bless you, sir."

"Who is this man?" he asked her.

She rolled her eyes skyward. "Leo James is bad man," she said. *Malo hombre.* "He buys horses and sells to Army. You go with him, yes?"

Tracker nodded.

"My Felipe do not trust him," she whispered. "You watch."

"Thanks, Maria," Tracker said. "Thanks for the food, for everything."

She smiled at him a warm smile that touched him somehow. She said softly, "Go with God, sir."

He gave her a bleak grin and went out into the night. Something moved beside the door, and the gun magically appeared in Tracker's hand.

"Hey, dammit, it's me," James swore.

Tracker laughed shortly. "You're liable to get shot sneaking around like that."

"Shore touchy," James grumbled. Suspiciously, he asked, "Ain't on the dodge, air you?"

Tracker said, "No more than you are." He mounted the gray. James, following him, stood beside the horse looking up at him.

"What's eatin' you, man?" he asked. "Why not tell me? Mebbe I could help you."

"Nothing bothering me that a hundred head of horses and five thousand dollars couldn't cure," Tracker said.

James whistled and then fell silent.

Tracker could feel that he waited for him to continue. He thought, *Why not?* Maybe it would

29

help to spill his guts some. It'd sure been bottled up, and sometimes he felt it eating away at his insides. He said, "I got a horse ranch up near Flagstaff. I needed help and didn't have the money to hire a man. So I took a partner."

James made a low noise that could have been a chuckle.

Tracker reached for his tobacco sack and fashioned a cigaret. He scratched a match on the saddle and the gray jumped. Sam Tracker's face was hard and bitter in the yellow light of the match. Sweat beaded his face.

"I had five thousand I borrowed on my place. This other fellow I took in, Kirby Landers, put in two thousand. He was supposed to be a real horse wrangler, knew horses, and what was more important he let on he had connections with the Army purchasing officer."

He thought of Kirby Landers then, and the vision of the man made his stomach ball up into a hard knot and rage rose in him. Good-looking Kirby, with his handstitched boots and fifty dollar Stetson. The man whom everybody liked, the man who had a way with the girls at the Saturday night dances. The man he'd given his friendship to—he tossed his cigaret away. He didn't say anything about Christine. He couldn't. That was the bitterest blow of all; Kirby had taken his girl, too. Christy, the girl who'd promised to marry him.

"Kirby was my friend, I thought, and I trusted him. We put our dough in the bank and . . ."

"Friend Landers grabbed it and vamoosed," James finished with a chuckle.

"How'd you figure that?" Tracker asked.

James was silent and then he said seriously, "You got a lead on this Kirby maybe? He's in Mule Creek, huh?"

"I don't know. He passed this way. Even if he hadn't headed in this direction I'd be here anyway. I got to have money to operate with. I know a man there who'll stake me."

"Maria told me you'd been shot," James said.

"Uh-huh," Tracker said coolly. "Landers did it. I nearly caught up with him."

James shivered. "I'm glad it wasn't me," he said. "Who's your man in Mule Creek?"

Tracker leaned from the saddle. "Friend, you want to know too damn much. You want me to ride for you or not?"

"Just thinkin'," James said. "That's a right smart bunch o' money for a man to dig up."

"He's got it," Tracker said, thinking of Jess Hamilton. "We rode together a lot of years back. He saved my life—and I've done a favor or two for him."

"He know you're comin'?"

"No." Tracker stood up in his stirrups. "Damn it, if you're through pumping me, let's go."

James grunted and moved off into the darkness.

31

In a moment his bulk reared up in the night atop the off-leader and he called out, "All right, let's move 'em."

The horses moved ahead on the road to Mule Creek.

The light in Maria's shack winked out. *Good woman,* he thought, *and just when I'd got to thinking maybe there weren't any left.* He felt a sense of gratitude to Maria Ortiz. He didn't think he'd forget her. It was more than her care and sympathy at a time when he was ready to break.

The moon came up, a brilliant yellow ball, edging over the dark rim of the distant mountains behind them. Tracker could see the bulk of the big man ahead through a haze of dust. He moved his neckerchief up over his mouth and nose, and settled his body to the motion of his mount.

For the first time he allowed himself to think about Christine Benton.

Maria had made it possible for him to think about Christine. It was hard to realize that the woman who'd told him she loved him, that she'd be his wife, had gone with Kirby. It was like a blast of thunder out of a clear blue sky. It wasn't possible and yet it had happened. He tried not to blame Christy, because, in spite of his love for her, he'd always realized that she usually went the way the wind blew. She had fallen under Kirby's spell just as a lot of other people had, including himself.

He knew little of Kirby's past—only that the

man had a lot of personal magnetism. He was one of those men who got along well in the world, even though his actions were not always on the right side. He was the type of man, Tracker thought, who as a boy did mischievous deeds and was smiled on by those in authority. Thinking back, he remembered that Kirby had cheated an old retired cavalry sergeant in a horse trade. The men around town had laughed about it. Tracker remembered them, bellying up to the bar, talking about it in terms that were not harmful at all to Kirby. That hadn't hurt him in the least. Another man, a lesser man, would have drawn their scorn, their disapproval.

He shook his head wonderingly. How was it that one man could do something and win approval and another man doing the very same thing drew the opposite reaction? They'd even thought it a sort of joke that Christine had run off with Kirby. He cursed mentally and loosened his fingers from the saddle horn. Damn it, why did he have to dredge that up out of his memories? He'd put Christine somewhere deep in his mind, and he meant for her to stay there.

Somewhere on the road, about midnight, James called a halt and dismounted from the off-leader. He staggered a little as he came back to where Tracker sat the gray in stony silence.

"Better have anosher drinksh," James said, and handed the bottle up to Tracker.

It was nearly empty. Tracker stood up in his stirrups and threw the bottle as hard as he could. He didn't hear it land in the soft sand off the road.

"What'd you do that for?" cried James. "There's a coupla drinks left in that bottle."

Tracker dismounted. "You're drunk now," he said. "Another drink and you'd go to sleep, and I don't know the road."

James was silent for a long moment, his resentment bubbling. He put it down because of what lay ahead. He said, "If we're gonna have any trouble, it'll be just down the road a little piece."

"Trouble? What kind of trouble?" Tracker fumbled for the makings. He fashioned a cigaret, and when he lighted it James hadn't answered. Tracker held up the match briefly and in its light saw that James's face was a pale, pasty gray.

"You hadn't ought to be showin' a light," he said.

Tracker shook out the match. "What're you scared of, James?"

" 'Paches. Little bunch broke outta th' reservation and are raisin' hell. They like Army hosses."

"They do," Tracker agreed. "That ten dollars cover this?"

"We get through without losin' any, I'll give you a hundred more," James said hurriedly.

Tracker was silent.

"I'll give you a hoss, too. Not one o' these, but a good one."

"What do you expect, and what're you going to do about it?" Tracker asked. He dropped his cigaret, grinding it out beneath his boot heel.

"The road goes through a little draw up ahead," James said. "If they're gonna jump us, it'll be there. If they do, we'll make a run for it. That's why I got the hosses rigged like this. Can run hell out of 'em and still keep 'em together."

Tracker nodded. He'd suspected something behind the rig James was using. But the man still hadn't told him the truth.

"All right," he said, "now you can stop lying."

"Aw, what d'you mean?"

"You know what I mean. Those five Apaches who broke off the reservation aren't going to bother anyone. Not any more."

"These are a bunch o' half-breeds," James said, and his voice was sullen.

"All right," said Tracker, after a short silence. He stepped up into his saddle. "Let's get 'em moving."

James looked up at him and chuckled deep in his throat and then turned and lumbered off. In a short while he called back, "Let's go."

They came into the shallow draw at a trot. The ground was hard here, where the wind had swept the rocks bare. There wasn't any dust, either. They went up a rise and the draw turned and narrowed. They got well into the narrow stretch, and ahead Tracker could see it spread out into a small valley. A red eye winked through the darkness.

Tracker heard a hoarse yell from ahead. It was James. "Get 'em runnin'," he screeched. "Get 'em goin' hard!"

Tracker spurred the gray and beat at its mate with his hat. The horses broke into a pounding gallop, and behind him Tracker could hear the wagon bouncing and rattling. The wagon scared the horses into an even harder run. Tracker hoped that the light wagon wouldn't turn over.

A dark mass moved up on his right, and at that moment he saw the red embers of a campfire. The dark mass moved away. It was a horse herd. The campfire blazed up as someone threw on fuel.

He caught a glimpse of a man rolling out of a blanket and a gun boomed in the night. Then they were past the campfire and out in the darkness. The horses, frightened, kept running. Tracker gradually pulled them down to a canter, a trot and then halted them.

"What're you stoppin' for?" James called fretfully.

Tracker cut the gray loose and rode up ahead and stopped beside James. "That herd back there," he said quietly. "I'm going to have a look at the brands. If I can catch one."

"You better not," James said. "You go back there somebody's liable to take a shot at you."

Tracker looked at him a moment and then shrugged. "Maybe he'll miss," he said quietly, and turned his horse. He called over his shoulder, as he rode away, "Don't move this cavvy 'til I come back, James."

CHAPTER 3

Tracker put the horse off the road and went up the slight incline of the ridge above where they'd brought the herd through. He didn't give a hang about leaving Leo James with the horse herd. The man was wrong, dead wrong and it wasn't just those shifty eyes that told him the story. James had lied to him for some reason.

He loosened his gun in the holster. There was a steady beat of his heart, quickening with excitement of imminent discovery. The soft, warm wind was on his face, as the gray took the rise willingly. He drew up and listened, and off to his left he heard the sound of a walking horse.

He put the gray over there and the outline of the horse loomed up and began drifting away from him. He put spurs to the gray and lunged in and grabbed the hackamore. The horse tried to pull loose and Tracker spoke a few soothing words and quieted it.

He got down from the gray and looped the reins around his left arm as he scratched a match alight. The horse jerked away as the match flared. Tracker talked again, quieting the animal as he looked at the brand. It was a Lazy A, a brand unknown to him. Disappointment filled him as he shook out the match and took the lariat from the saddle. He tied it on to the hackamore and began

38

cruising the ridge, picking up a horse here and there. When he got back to where the campfire was located he had a dozen horses on his string.

He sat his horse looking out into the darkness. He could hear the sound of running horses out there, and knew that the wrangler was gathering the stampeded stock. He shook his head. It was a near hopeless task in the darkness. He got down from the gray and walked the horses over to the pepper trees surrounding a spring. He bumped into a rope, burning his hand where it raked along the lariat. Horses moved beyond the rope corral. They'd gathered a few at least.

He tied the gray and looped the lariat around the single strand rope of the makeshift corral and went back to the ashes of the fire. There were a few sticks of wood there and he squatted, feeding bits of wood into the ashes until it flared up. He added a few sticks and stood up stretching, when he heard the distinctive metallic click of a gun being cocked.

He froze.

"That's right," a voice said. "Just stand real quiet and don't make any sudden move."

For an instant he felt like diving off and trying for his gun, but the click of that cocked gun was still in his ears. All the man had to do was twitch his trigger finger.

The man circled him, holding the pistol aimed at the upper part of Tracker's body. At that range he couldn't miss. He was a stocky, slope-shouldered man with a brown face covered with bristly gray whiskers. His eyes slitted with anger, he cursed roundly. "Ain't got enough he'p to swing you for a horse thief," he said venomously, "but I could put a bullet through you easy enough."

"You got it all wrong, friend," Tracker said, quietly enough. He wondered if James would return, but at once knew he wouldn't. He wasn't the kind of man to help another unless there was something in it for him. "I just gathered a few of your horses." He nodded toward the string he'd tied to the rope corral.

"Don't sound right to me." The man spoke angrily with no uncertainty in his voice. "I ain't about to kill a man in cold blood, but by damn I feel like doin' it right now."

"You got some cause," Tracker acknowledged. "But believe me, I was trying to help you."

A horse moved up out of the darkness and a slight figure slipped from the bareback animal. "I got one more, and I guess that's about . . ." She stopped speaking and stared at Tracker. She was a young girl; he could tell that, from her face. She wore a floppy old black hat, a rough shirt and a pair of wool pants stuffed into half boots. She gazed from Tracker to the gun and back again. "Who's he?"

"Says he gathered up some hosses," the man muttered. "That's what he says."

"Put the gun away," Tracker said.

"He don't look like a horse thief to me," the girl said.

"What does a horse thief look like?" the man asked cynically.

"There's a dozen horses there," the girl said. "Why would he bring them in here if he was trying to steal them?"

The man lowered the gun and then shoved it into the half-breed holster. He said, "I'm so all-fired damn mad I guess I didn't know what I was doin'."

The girl sat back in the sand looking at Tracker in frank appraisal.

Tracker moved closer to the fire and squatted there and the man squatted across from him and they all stared at one another. The wind dusted sand across the fire.

"My name's Tracker. Sam Tracker."

"Frank Cady," the man said. He gestured to the girl. "My gal, Pat. What happened here tonight?"

"I guess I spooked your horses," Tracker said.

"You did?" Cady's face hardened. "You better do some talkin'."

"I didn't know what I was doing," Tracker admitted. "I was helping a man get a herd to Mule Creek. He told me there might be a bunch of half-breeds camped here at the spring. Expected they might take his horses."

Cady looked into the fire, biting at his lip, his

eyes slitted. "I reckon you must be workin' for Leo James."

"The same. Know him?"

Cady snorted. "Know him? For an egg-suckin' dog . . ."

"Papa," Pat Cady said warningly.

"What the hell you doin' here?" Cady glared at him.

"I thought to help you gather them up," Tracker said. "I feel responsible. If I'd known . . ."

"Leo ought to be in jail," Cady said bitterly.

"What's it all about?" Tracker asked.

"He's tryin' to get to Mule Creek before I do."

"I guess I'm just a dumb horse wrangler," Tracker said mildly. "I don't figure how that would do him much good."

Pat Cady moved out into the darkness and returned with a smoke-blackened coffee pot. She placed it in the hot coals and used a stick to rake more coals around it. Then she left again and returned with a frying pan and a few boiled potatoes. She knelt before the fire and began peeling the skins off the potatoes and slicing them into the pan.

Cady searched his pockets until he found a rumpled cigar. He carefully licked the broken leaves into place and picked a burning twig from the small fire and touched off his smoke. He sat down, leaned back on his elbows and blew smoke at the sky. "There's reason enough, Tracker. You see the Army buys all the right kind of hosses they can get. Just can't seem to get enough."

"I've dealt with them," Tracker said.

Cady nodded. "Yeah—well, the Army works in funny ways, Tracker. They only buy so many hosses each month, on account of a funny somethin' they call stretchin' the budget. They're right down to the point where they ain't gonna buy for a couple o' weeks now."

"I see what you mean," Tracker said thoughtfully. "The man who brings in horses after the next bunch gets there'll have to hold them."

"You got it," Cady said. "An' holdin' hosses in Mule Creek ain't no simple proposition. No graze. And you gotta buy feed. You even gotta pay for a place to keep 'em unless you want to keep a wrangler on twenty-four hours a day to keep 'em from strayin' or gettin' stole. There's a hoss thief behind every cactus since the Army stepped up its heavy buyin'."

Tracker glanced at the girl, warming potatoes in the skillet over the fire. She returned his look with guileless blue eyes. He had thought she was a young girl; but kneeling there before the fire, he could see she had the fully developed curves of maturity. It was an effort to pull his gaze back to Cady. "I guess maybe I better stay with you until the horses are gathered."

Cady shook his head. "It's nice of you to think of it," he said. "But I couldn't beat James in even with your help. He's out ahead now. I might just hold 'em here at the springs until I talk to Major O'Donnel. Maybe he'll stretch that damn red tape and take 'em."

"I'll help," Tracker said. "I feel obligated to do it."

"An' maybe you just wanna hang around my gal," Cady said coldly.

"Papa," the girl spoke sharply, her skin flushing red. "You better hush that kind of talk."

Tracker rose, his bleak face breaking into a smile. "Ain't such a bad idea at that," he said. "Well, I'll help you if you want. If not, I'll get on back to James."

"Thank you just the same," Cady said without rising.

Tracker wheeled and started for the gray. He stopped as Cady called him.

"I do thank you," Cady said earnestly. "I just wouldn't want you to get crossways with that rotten outfit in Mule Creek."

"Papa, you better hush. You know how things get out."

Tracker waited patiently, not interfering in the father-daughter differences.

"This one won't do any talkin'," Cady said. He rose and stepped around the fire, closer to Tracker. "You'll learn it sooner or later. Leo James is Arnie True's right hand."

"I just met Leo James," Tracker said. "And I wouldn't know Arnie True from Adam's off ox."

"He's a snake-eyed breed," Cady said venomously. "He runs Mule Creek and just about everything in his part o' the country. You or anybody wanna do anything in Mule Creek you gotta clear it with Arnie."

"You stop that kind of talk," Pat Cady said.

"You clearing anything with Arnie?"

Cady grinned with humor. "Listen, Tracker, I clear nothin' with nobody."

"Then how come . . ."

The stocky man touched the gun at his hip. "I used to be an Arizona Ranger," he said. "I still got lots o' friends in the Rangers. Arnie'll take on the U. S. Army before he'd take on the Rangers. He knows me and lets me alone."

"Thanks for tipping me, Cady," Tracker said. He looked at Pat Cady and touched his hat.

"You better have something to eat before you go," Pat Cady called to him.

Tracker looked at Cady for confirmation and the man nodded grudgingly. Sam Tracker shook his head. "Thanks, ma'am, but I'll get along." He untied the gray, stepped in the saddle and headed out into the night. He felt guilty about stampeding Cady's horses and he'd have liked to help the man. But there was no giving on Cady's part. He was one of that rare breed of men who are reluctant to accept favors because they find it binding. If a man did Cady a favor, he wouldn't rest until it was returned with interest. Tracker grinned in the darkness. Damned if that wasn't how he felt himself.

He reached the top of the ridge and trotted the horse on down to where Leo James waited. The fat man was prowling up and down; he stomped impatiently out to meet Tracker.

"What the hell kept you?" he demanded.

Tracker swung down and said, "I ought to knock your head off."

James grinned. "Hell, man, you got a hundred an' a horse comin'. Whatcha kickin' about?"

"You knew who that was."

"Maybe I did, maybe I didn't. Let's get these bangtails movin'." He moved off toward the head of the string.

Tracker started after him and then shrugged, hitching the gray back into the string. He mounted and called, "I'm ready when you are."

"Then let's move 'em out," James hollered.

The long hitch moved ahead through the night.

They traveled slowly, for the horses were tired. The sky behind Tracker lightened and the landscape was revealed. Riding along the slope, the terrain fell away slowly to a flatland and in the distance was a cluster of trees. The horses moved faster without urging.

A stillness was all around as they rode into Mule Creek. The town was asleep, its false-fronted stores shuttered. A lone piebald cow pony stood head-down at the hitchrail in front of the Bird

Cage Saloon; its owner slumped on the boardwalk.

They went through the town, the rumble of hooves loud between the buildings, the sound scattering on the vacant lots. James pulled up the off-leader at a rundown corral on the river bank. James got down and came back, stretching, yawning, and rubbing his face with his hands. "That does it," he said with satisfaction in his voice.

Tracker stepped to the ground, his legs feeling the cramp of the ride. His throat was dry, his canteen having been empty for the last four hours. He was hungry and tired, and he still felt a streak of anger burning in him for James's treachery.

"Hope you're satisfied," he said sourly.

James grinned, showing short stained teeth. "What're you kickin' about, horse wrangler?"

"When I start kicking you'll know it," Tracker replied.

"Help me turn 'em in the corral and I'll buy your breakfast."

Tracker silently unhooked the horses, two at a time, and turned them into the corral. When he finished, James was forking hay over the bars to the hungry animals. The sun was well up, and smoke rose from a few tumbledown shacks across the river. Back of him, toward town, Tracker could hear the clanging ring of a hammer on an anvil as an early-starting blacksmith began work.

James waddled out of the corral. A few wisps of hay clung to his clothing. "I gotta see a fellar. You come with me. Then we'll eat."

"I'll get breakfast," Tracker said, "and meet you right here."

James made an impatient gesture. "Won't take long," he said. "An' I wancha to meet this fellar."

"What for?"

"Durn, but you're touchy. I jes' wancha to meet him. He might be able to help you one way or another."

Tracker shrugged. "Let's go, then."

They walked together toward the town. The sun was hot now, bearing down with what promised to be a scorching day.

James turned into an alleyway between the Bird Cage and a harness shop and went back into the warm dimness. He halted for a moment before a closed door, his pudgy face serious. He knocked hesitantly.

"Well, come on in, you mucklehead!" a hoarse voice called from beyond the door.

Tracker was struck by James's evident fear. The look on his face bordered on terror. He didn't have time to speculate further, for James pushed open the door.

"Hello, Arnie," he said ingratiatingly. He held up his hand to a half-bald man with a skull-like face who sat behind a roll top desk.

"You finally got here?"

"Just as fast as I could," James said in a quaking whine.

The bald man stood up quickly and his hand went out, pointing to Tracker. "Who's that?"

Tracker had a look at the man's eyes and he knew why James was scared. There was a fearful quality in the man James called Arnie. His face, thin and bony, was touched with evil. His black eyes were hooded, unwinking, watchful, beady as a snake.

Tracker glanced contemptuously at James as the man attempted placation. "Good grannies, Arnie, I wouldn't be here now except fer him. He gimme a hand with the horses."

"Well?"

"Shoot, Arnie, excuse me. This here is Sam Tracker."

Tracker saw True's eyes flicker and wondered what it meant, if anything. True said, "Tracker," and dismissed him, swinging his head back to James, his fingers moving impatiently over the desk.

"How many?"

"Many's I could get," James said eagerly. "Forty head, Arnie, all prime."

While Tracker was wondering why James didn't mention the incident on the trail, there were light steps beyond an inner door, and then someone tapped lightly. The door swung open at True's command and a tall girl entered. She stopped just inside the door, hesitating. She had a direct look without being bold, Tracker thought. Her dark and wavy hair was upswept, and her plain, dark clothing couldn't conceal the clean lines of her splendid body.

Tracker found her dark eyes on him, and there was disapproval in them at his stare. He moved his feet and the board under him creaked.

"I didn't know you had visitors," she told True. "Jason Andrews wants to see you, and he said he was in a hurry."

Her voice was throaty, husky, and caused Tracker to thrill strangely. He saw no rings on her fingers. Her ankles peeping from the long dark dress were shapely.

True looked at Tracker and then back to the girl. "I'll see him in a minute," he said and added to Tracker, "Wait here." He went to still another door, opened it, and motioned James in with his head. James went on reluctant feet through the door and it closed on the two of them. Tracker was alone with the girl.

She walked to the desk and straightened a few papers. She didn't look directly at him.

"You work for Mr. True?"

"Yes, I do." She always wondered at the directness of the men she'd come in contact with in this barren country. This one seemed a shade different from most of the dusty riders who came through Arnie True's rear door, but he must be like the others. These thoughts ran swiftly through her mind as she studied him covertly.

"You like working here?"

Her hands stopped moving over the desk and she stood very still for a moment. Then she gave him an amused smile and nodded.

He could sense that she didn't mean it. What in hell, he wondered, was a girl like her doing in a place like this?

Voices came to them from beyond the wall. True was shouting, but Tracker couldn't make out what he was saying. He looked at the girl. Her smooth oval face was pale and he saw that her hands trembled. She tried to hide them in the folds of her skirts.

Tracker felt uncomfortable. "Say, Miss—Miss . . ."

"Rainey," she said faintly. "Jean Rainey."

"Mine's Tracker. Sam Tracker. Is Jason Andrews a horse trader, too?"

She nodded. "Yes. Why do you ask?"

"There seems to be a lot of them around here," he said grimly. "Do you know anyone named Kirby Landers?" He watched her face closely as he spoke the name.

He didn't get an answer. The door flew open, and James slunk in, followed closely by Arnie True. James didn't stop, but jerked his chin toward the door, his face white and sweaty.

Tracker followed him out, glancing once at the

girl. She stood there in the middle of the room, her hands clutched to her breast. It was a picture that stayed with him. Everyone around True seemed to be terrified.

In an eating place called simply The Chinaman's, down the street, a Mexican woman took their order and brought them strong black coffee to drink while they waited for their ham and eggs to cook.

"Well, I met him," Tracker observed. "He didn't seem overjoyed when he saw me."

"Aw, well, Arnie was a mite upset. I was a coupla days late."

"Don't crawfish, Leo," Tracker said. "You were plain damn scared to go in there alone and you know it."

"Aw, shoot," James said and looked relieved as the Mexican woman put their plates on the table. He scooped up a mouthful of egg and the yolk dribbled on his chin. "You don't connect up with this friend o' yours," he went on as he wolfed his food, "mebbe I can help you out."

"Who you want killed?" Tracker asked.

The fat man frowned heavily. Then his frown disappeared as he chuckled, "You're funnin'. I got a lil job that needs doin'. Maybe you'd like it anyway."

Tracker shook his head. "Just that horse you promised—and the hundred dollars."

"Easiest money you ever earned," James said.

He put his knife and fork beside his plate and laboriously took out his purse. He counted out five twenty-dollar gold eagles and shoved them over to Tracker.

Tracker drained his coffee and stood up, pocketing the money.

James paid for their breakfast and they walked back toward the corral beside the river. "Who's the tall girl in True's office?"

"Hee, hee, ain't she a looker?" James chortled. "Funny thing about that gal. She does some book work for Arnie."

"What's funny about her?" Tracker wanted to know.

James emitted the chuckle that Tracker was beginning to hate. "Arnie brought her out from Kansas City fur to entertain in the Bird Cage. Guess she thought it was opery 'er somethin 'til she got here. She didn't like it. Quit the next day. Boys all crazy about her, too. An' she quit!"

"She's working now to get enough money to go back East," Tracker conjectured aloud. "Guess she's the proud kind."

"That's about it," James agreed. He sighed. "Man, she's some gal."

Tracker felt like hitting him.

They turned into the corral and Tracker got his saddle from the light wagon. James brought out a fair-looking horse, a short-coupled bay, as compact as a balled fist.

"This'n do?" asked James, his small black eyes leering at Tracker.

Tracker nodded. "The Army wouldn't take him, but he'll do for me," he said.

The smile left James's face. "What's wrong with that gelding?" he challenged.

Tracker laid his hand on the bay's hip. "Capped hip," he said. "Must of fallen when he was a colt. But that wouldn't keep him off my string."

There was respect in James's voice when he said, "You sure know horses."

Tracker saddled the bay and stepped in the saddle. He looked down at James. "You got me a horse and a hundred ten bucks," he said. "I should feel grateful."

James simply grinned at him. "You don't get what you're after," he said, "drop by and see me. I got a deal for you."

Tracker didn't answer. He looked back when he reined in at the blacksmith shop and saw James still standing there, staring after him. He tried to shrug away the chill that centered suddenly in his spine.

CHAPTER 4

Arnold True smiled his thin lipless smile at Jean Rainey. That smile never failed to chill her but she didn't reveal it.

"Hold Jason up," he said. "I want to see Shag and Dub first."

She said, "Yes, sir, Mr. True," and turned and walked from the room, with Arnie watching the movement of her body. She was aware of his gaze because it seemed to go right through her. But she didn't reveal her awareness of that either. It was as if by ignoring a threat it would go away of its own accord.

True filled a pipe, placed it in his mouth and scratched a match alight and touched it to the pipe. He puffed it afire and carefully shook out the match and sat down. He leaned back in his chair, pulling in the smoke and letting it rise slowly from his open mouth. He'd vented his small anger on Leo James and he felt only a slight discontent, which was normal.

Arnold True, the illegitimate son of a cavalry sergeant, had risen high in his world. His Apache mother had let him grow up without training or restraint. He had learned his own set of basic rules for living back at the Army post where he was born. For a man skilled at following them, they made life as simple as taking a horse to water.

Essentially it was only one rule: the whole world is the enemy, but don't let on that it is. When you have to fight, fight with everything you've got, but only when the enemy isn't expecting it or doesn't know what's coming next. Never let yourself get boxed in.

Above all, never let another living person know what you're thinking or what you're doing.

The formula had worked for True. He was in his prime at forty, well-to-do, a power in Apache County, a success as measured by the standards of the country. He followed the rules, but he knew they worked only if you followed them in everything—even so small a thing as checking on a cold-eyed, competent-appearing stranger, a newcomer.

The door opened and two slim, granite-faced, blank-eyed men stalked in. They might have been brothers. They were dressed alike—black, flat-crowned hats, dark shirts, black pants, and black-butted guns on thigh, hung low and tied down. Shag Wiltse had a small black mustache and Dub Crewe was blind in one eye, his left eye a milky gray from some childhood accident.

"There's a new man in town." True spoke from his lipless mouth after the smoke was gone. "Tracker. See what he's here for, what he's up to."

The duo didn't speak. Wiltse nodded and went toward the door that opened on the alley; Crewe followed without even nodding.

Arnold True sat there for a moment and then he walked across the room and opened the inside door and said, "Jason, come on in."

Tracker found out from a friendly blacksmith that he'd have to retrace part of his tracks of the night before to reach the Rafter H. He decided to visit the remount station first. He went out the south road that angled toward the river and came on the twin adobes that headquartered the officer in charge and his small crew.

He tied up in front of the largest adobe, walked over to the corral and looked at the horses behind the rails. He saw now that the corral was built out into the river so the horses could drink. A shelter made of brush was in one corner; and several horses stood in the shade of it.

He turned, walked to the adobe and went in through the open door. An enlisted man rose from the table inside the door. "Can I help you, sir?" he asked.

"I'd like to speak to the commanding officer," Tracker said.

"Major O'Donnel," the orderly said. "I'll see, sir." He moved to an inner door and knocked. When a deep voice answered, he opened the door and went in. There was a murmur of talk, then the orderly stepped through the door and motioned Sam Tracker in.

Major Kelvin O'Donnel was a man grown old in

the service. He had gray-blond hair. He was standing at his desk, erect, with his stomach pulled in to hide his paunchiness. His face was reddened with a rupturing of blood vessels in his cheeks. He gave Tracker a frosty stare and blinked his agate eyes, screened with bushy eyebrows the same color as his hair.

"I don't believe I have the pleasure," he said, and as an afterthought, added, "sir."

"My name is Sam Tracker. I run a horse ranch up near Flagstaff."

A glimmer of recognition flashed in the hard agate eyes. "I remember the name," he said, offering his hand.

They shook hands.

"O'Donnel," said the major, and motioned to a seat beside his desk. "Sit down, Tracker." He sat down himself, opened a box of cigars and offered it to Tracker. "What brings you to this godforsaken part of the country?" He struck a match on the underside of his desk, then leaned forward to give Tracker a light.

"Horses," Tracker said.

"That's my business," Major O'Donnel said wryly. He leaned back in his chair. "You usually deal with Prescott, don't you?"

"I've been talking with them," Tracker admitted. "I lost a bunch of horses and I trailed them this far."

The major's chair came forward with a rush.

"Stolen horses? I'd never buy a horse, Tracker, that I didn't know where it came from."

Tracker stared at him without speaking.

"I've been out here long enough to know what goes on. I've had a chance to pick up horses we'd normally pay a hundred and fifty dollars for, for a gold eagle." He shook his head. "I made a hard and fast rule that when I pay out tax money for a horse it's not going to be to some thief."

"That's a mighty fine rule," Tracker said.

Blood mounted angrily in O'Donnel's face; he'd made too much of a speech and he realized it. "Tracker, you know how the Army operates. I couldn't afford to let a breath of scandal get back to Prescott. The very thought of it sort of sent me sounding off. You understand?"

Tracker nodded. "Do you buy horses from a Mr. True?"

"I buy horses from any reliable source," snapped the major.

Tracker studied O'Donnel's anger, then laughed. "Major, don't let my simple questions get you rattled."

O'Donnel got up and turned his back on Tracker and walked to the window. He stared out at the hardpacked corral shimmering in the heat. "I'm up for retirement," he said. "Just a year to go before my pension. I can't let anything happen that would spoil that, Tracker. I've put in too many hard years to let anything upset it. Do you understand why I'm so all-fired careful?"

"I never met an Army officer yet who wasn't careful," Tracker said.

O'Donnel turned. "I sense a note of derogation."

"Not at all," Tracker said. "You're interested in preserving your pension. I'm interested in getting back my horses which were stolen. You insist that it's impossible for a questionably owned horse to be purchased here. I insist that if you deal with a man named Leo James or . . ."

"Don't say Arnold True," O'Donnel said quietly. "Please don't say that name in connection with stolen horses. It could kill you, Tracker."

"Just between you and me?" Tracker asked in amusement.

Major O'Donnel shook his head. "You can't open your mouth in Apache County without True knowing about it."

"There's one trooper out there," Tracker said. "Your orderly. Don't you trust him?"

"Don't ask me how he does it," O'Donnel said. "Of course I trust my orderly." He moved back to his desk and sat down again. "If it'll help, I'll keep my eyes open. What brand should I look for?"

"T-Bar," Tracker said, rising. "Thanks for the cigar, Major. Maybe we'll meet again sometime."

O'Donnel was silent, sitting there, watching him walk across the room and through the door.

Tracker mounted the bay and rode across

country, toward the Rafter H, his mind busy with Major Kelvin O'Donnel. The major was a frightened man. What did he have to hide? Tracker's first thought was that O'Donnel might be involved with the questionable purchase of Army mounts. But he couldn't be sure. In his dealings with Army officers at Prescott, he'd run into some excessively prudent men. Maybe the major was one of those who grew faint at the idea of making a decision; the Army was full of them.

His thoughts drifted from O'Donnel to Jess Hamilton, the man he was riding to see. Sam Tracker had made a prospecting trip into the Sangre de Cristos to make a stake for the ranch. He was well on his way to a nice sack of gold dust when the Apaches fell on him. He was holding them off when Hamilton, then a civilian scout for General George Crook, took a hand. Tracker remembered the fight with a slight smile, but he hadn't felt like smiling when it was happening. Afterward, he split his dust with Hamilton. That's how Hamilton got the stake to go ranching.

The trail led north and there was level land all around, with clumps of trees marking the waterholes. Here and there the bear grass grew in clumps, and cattle dotted the landscape. It was still desert country, but with a difference. There was water here, not in abundance, but sufficient for the purpose.

For some reason that he didn't take the trouble

to define, Tracker felt buoyant and lighthearted for the first time since taking to Kirby Landers' trail. He lifted his voice in song so loud that the short-coupled bay twitched his ears and began dancing. Tracker patted his neck. "Don't like that, hey?" he asked aloud. "Well, it ain't like I was an oprey singer, hoss. You gotta stand it, just like you gotta take me places. It's all part of being a hoss, see?"

He grinned at his own foolishness and put the bay through his paces. He settled on a mile-eating lope that the horse seemed to like.

The Rafter H was an imposing spread. Tracker came through the big gate, a mile from the ranch buildings which squatted in a cluster of trees. A wrought-iron H under a rafter was in the arch above the gate. Fat steers grazed along the wagon road. As he neared the ranch, a long-eared hound came baying, and the cook showed briefly in the door of the cookshack, which was a lean-to adjoining the bunkhouse.

Tracker tried the office first, and, when he'd knocked a second time the cook came outside his shack and hollered, "Ain't nobody home but me."

Leading the bay, Tracker walked over to the cookshack and hauled up. "I'm looking for Jess Hamilton."

"Jess an' some o' the boys are pushing a herd up in the hills. Ought t' be back by sundown."

"I'm a friend of Jess's," Tracker said. "We met

up when he was scouting for Crook some years back."

The cook scratched his graying chin whiskers thoughtfully. "Jess's great feller," he said. "Better light and have a snack while you wait."

"Wouldn't mind a cup of coffee," Tracker said, then tied the bay to a cottonwood and followed the cook into the kitchen. It was a big room, light and open, clean with a big black range on which a stew was simmering.

The cook pushed a broken-backed chair up to his work table and nodded for Tracker to sit down.

Tracker dropped his hat on the floor and turned the chair and straddled it. "That stew smells good."

"It's about ready," the cook said. "Wanta try a bowl?"

"No, thanks. But I'd sure like a couple of those doughnuts."

The cook poured a cup of coffee, placed two doughnuts on a saucer, and placed them on the table. He wiped his hands on his apron and finished loading a tray he'd apparently been working on when Tracker arrived.

"I gotta take this up to the big house," he said, picking up the tray. "Be back in just a few minutes."

Tracker bit into the doughnut and nodded without speaking. The doughnuts were good and he finished them and drank coffee. He got another doughnut from the big dishpan that was heaping with them and was almost finished when the cook returned.

"Somebody sick?" Tracker asked.

The cook poured himself a cup of coffee and carried it to the table and sat down near Tracker. "Yep," he announced importantly. "A gal. Boss found her on the Mule Creek trail. Ain't really sick. Just saddle wore, plumb to a frazzle."

"How'd she come to be out there?"

The cook shook his head mournfully at the vagaries of mankind. "She was travelin' with some feller and he ditched her. Guess she was slowin' him down some."

A dreadful thought flashed through Tracker's mind. "What's her name?" he asked slowly.

"Christine Benton," the cook said. "Real purty, hair like a new lariat and eyes blue as daisies, skin the color o' canned cream . . ." He broke off as he looked up to see Tracker disappearing through the doorway.

"Well, I'll be a doggone doggie," he said. "Whatever got into that cowboy?"

CHAPTER 5

Tracker strode toward the big house and his mind wasn't working at all. He couldn't seem to think; what thoughts he had were a wild jumble. A wild jumble of thoughts and a cold feeling in his guts.

He went quickly into the house and stood just inside the door, his eyes adjusting to the dimness. She sat in a rocking chair by the window, which was open, to catch some of the warm breeze that came through. He stood there and she continued to stare out the window, rocking gently, as though he wasn't there. The food tray stood on a small table beside her and the food had not been touched.

"I saw you ride up," she said. "I wanted to run out and throw myself in your arms. Then I wanted to dash upstairs and crawl under the bed like I used to do when I was a kid and there was a thunderstorm. But I didn't do anything. I just sat here hoping you'd go away."

He tramped slowly across the room and stood beside her chair, looking down at the soft gleam of her bright hair. The cook had said it was the color of a new lariat and Tracker saw that he was right, though he'd never thought of the comparison before. He said, "Where is he?"

She turned her head then, looking up at him. Her blue eyes were awash with tears, the pale oval of her face framed with her lustrous hair.

"He's not worth your bullet," she said.

"Let me decide that."

She rose suddenly and stepped close and put her arms around his neck and laid her cheek against his chest. "Sam, Sam," she whispered. "I'm so sorry. . . ." She cried.

He didn't try to keep her from crying. From the chaos of his thoughts some order sifted out. She was sorry. He was sorry for her. He was sorry she'd run away with Landers.

She pulled away and wiped her eyes and said, "I don't know what made me do it. He wanted me to go. Like a fool I agreed. When the going got tough he left me. He said you'd take care of me. He laughed when he said it."

"Where is he?" Sam asked again.

She shook her head. "I can't tell you, Sam."

He took her two arms and swung her around and shook her savagely. "Tell me where I can find him, Christy!"

His anger, he realized, was unreasonable. He tried to tell himself to take it easy, but the past days and nights had caught up with him. He heard the floor creak.

"Let the lady go, Mr. Tracker," said a soft voice.

He turned, dropping his hands to his side.

Two men stood inside the door, slim, lean men, with the stamp of gunfighter in their garb, in their actions. The one with the mustache said, "Run on upstairs, little lady."

Christine hesitated, looking at Tracker.

"Do what he says," Tracker warned and watched her as she walked slowly across the room. The man with the mustache watched her too. She went up the stairs and both men looked at Tracker.

When Christine's feet disappeared, and her slow steps went across the upstairs room, the two men moved in on Tracker, but not near enough for him to touch either of them.

"I didn't know Jess hired gunfighters," Tracker said.

"We just want to ask a few questions," said the milky-eyed one. "You answer them right and we'll be on our way."

"Then you don't work for Jess?" Tracker said. He didn't see the man on his left move, but the gun appeared somehow in his hand and slashed down on Tracker's skull, driving him to his knees.

"We'll ask the questions, *hombre*," murmured the mustached man. "I'm Wiltse and this is my partner, Crewe. You just speak when we put a question. We like the answer, fine. We don't like it, we hit you with a gun. We can last all day, *amigo*."

"Where you from?" Crewe asked.

"Near Flagstaff," Tracker said. He put his hand to his head and felt an egg-sized lump. He looked at his fingers, tinged with blood. "I own a horse ranch there." He slowly climbed to his feet.

"Wiltse, you think that's right?" Crewe asked.

Wiltse grinned. "Sounds right."

"What're you doin' here?" Crewe asked.

"To see an old friend. Jess Hamilton." Keep calm, he told himself. Don't do any damfoolery like trying to charge a pistol in the hands of a man who knows how to use it.

"Just to see him?" Crewe demanded. "Just a sociable visit, Tracker, and nothin' else?"

These two were not ignorant, run-of-the-mill gunfighters, Tracker realized. "I was going to borrow some money from him."

The two men looked at each other and then back to Tracker. "Hear that, Shag?" Crewe demanded with a grin.

"Yeah, real funny," Wiltse answered. Both of them began laughing.

"What's so funny?" Tracker demanded.

Wiltse stopped laughing and his eyes bored at Tracker. "What was you doin' out at the yellowlegs outfit?" He stepped forward and reached for Tracker's gun. Tracker swayed and the flat of his hand caught Wiltse squarely in the throat and his other hand swept the gun out of Wiltse's hand.

"Don't move!" his voice cracked at Crewe and the man froze with his hand inches from his gun. Wiltse writhed on the floor, his two hands clutching at his throat. Tracker leaned down without taking his eyes from Crewe and

68

unbuckled the gunbelt and jerked it free of the agony wracked body.

"Drop your gunbelt," Tracker said, motioning with Wiltse's gun. Crewe carefully unbuckled his gunbelt and let it fall to the floor. "Kick it over here," Tracker ordered.

Crewe said, "Listen, friend . . ."

"Shut up and do what you're told!"

Crewe kicked the gunbelt across the floor.

"Pick up your sidekick," Tracker ordered, "and get him in that chair."

Crewe rolled Wiltse over and put his arms through his armpits and half-dragged him to the chair and sat him in it.

Wiltse finally got his breath and groaned. "I'll kill you for that."

"If you don't get killed trying," Tracker said. "Now, what were you two braying about when I told you I wanted to borrow money from Hamilton?"

"Everybody knows Hamilton's a skinflint," Crewe grumbled.

"Who do you two work for?" Tracker asked. "Or maybe you're in business for yourself?"

Wiltse whispered, "You go to hell." Tears stood in his eyes and he had difficulty breathing, tugging at his throat.

When Tracker stepped forward with the gun raised, Crewe said hastily, "Wait a minute now. We work for True. That's no secret. Anybody can tell you."

"Why are you out here asking me questions about what I'm doing?"

"Arnie likes to know what goes on."

"You mean he questions every stranger who shows in Mule Creek?"

"That's about the size of it," Crewe said. He rubbed his jaw. "There ain't too many."

Tracker looked at them for a full minute. "All right," he said at last. "Get on your horses and get out of here."

"What about our guns?" Crewe demanded.

Tracker grinned. "I'll leave 'em with the bartender at the Bird Cage," he said.

"The hell you will," Wiltse shouted. "By gawd . . ."

"Shut up, Shag," Crewe said, tight-lipped. "Come on."

"That's being a smart boy," Tracker said, and the two looked at him with naked hate before they moved to the door. Tracker stood in the door watching them mount up and ride away. When they were out of pistol range they stopped, turned their horses, and Crewe yanked a saddle gun out of the boot, leveled it and put a bullet in the porch post.

Tracker felt the splinters hit his back as he plunged through the door. He looked around the room, searching for a rifle. There wasn't one. He ran through the short, dark hallway and into the kitchen as he heard another rifle slug hit the house with a thump and then the flat spang of the Winchester.

There was an old .50 Sharps standing in the corner. Tracker yanked it up. It was unloaded, and looked as though it hadn't been fired in years. He pulled open the kitchen table drawer and dumped the contents on the floor. No shells there. He ran to the cupboard and began emptying cans, boxes and anything that looked as though it might hold shells. He found three.

He grabbed them up, shoving one into the breech of the old single shooter. He went at a run back to the front of the house as another bullet thudded into the front wall. He knelt at the open window and shoved the Sharps through, sighted it, and pulled the trigger. The kick was fierce, but he saw dirt spurt up beneath Wiltse's horse. Before he could reload the two gunmen put spurs to their horses and galloped down the road. The long-barreled Sharps had them outgunned.

The two men were out of range by the time he got out on the porch.

As the gunmen dwindled in the distance, the old cook came cautiously up from the cookshack. "What'd them dry-gulchers want?"

"Don't know for sure," Tracker said. "They asked a few questions." He set the Sharps butt down on the porch, holding the barrel. "Packs quite a wallop, that old gun."

"That it does. Killed a sight of buffalo with it."

He squinted at Tracker. "What'n hell they shootin' at you fur?"

"I riled 'em, I guess," Tracker said. "Who are they?"

"Arnie True's guns. Know him?"

"I've met him," Tracker admitted.

"What'n tarnation did they want?" the cook asked again.

"They wanted to know where I'm from. They wanted to know what I'm doing here."

The old cook shook his head sadly. "That's like Arnie. He gets restless when a stranger shows up. He's got to know everything."

"I didn't hear the dog," Tracker said.

"For good reason. They come like Injuns. The dog's lyin' out there dead."

"I didn't hear a shot."

"Another good reason. They killed him with a knife."

"Do True's men usually go around acting like that?"

"Sure's my name's Curly York. They do just about what they damn well please and when they please. You gonna stay here or wait at the cookshack?"

"I'll stay here," Tracker said, "if you don't mind."

"I don't mind." The bald-headed man, whose name aptly enough was Curly, turned away, not trying to hide his disappointment. "The missy all right?"

"She's fine," Tracker said.

The cook trudged away. He was disappointed that Tracker didn't come down to keep him company. A cook on a ranch had few friends. The very nature of his business forbade friendship, for if you favored one, there was bound to be trouble. Curly York was a good man, a fair man, a poor cook. He tramped back toward the cookshack, pondering the fact that the hard-faced man, Sam Tracker, had attracted Arnie True's attention.

Tracker cleaned up the kitchen and put it in order from the confusion he'd created looking for shells. Christine was still upstairs when Jess Hamilton arrived. Tracker hadn't heard her and he had refrained from disturbing her.

He was standing on the porch when the big man reined up and dismounted. A squint-eyed redhead, Jess Hamilton hadn't changed any that Tracker could see. A cowhand eyed Tracker curiously as he led Hamilton's horse away.

Hamilton came up on the porch with a questioning look on his face.

"Jess," Tracker said, "you remember me?"

Jess Hamilton's red-brown face cleared and he put out a big hand. "Sam Tracker, by all that's holy!"

They shook hands and Hamilton pushed Tracker into the house and on into the kitchen.

"Sit down there," Jess said, "while I build a fire. My housekeeper left last week and I'm batching it." He lifted the stove lid, shoved a handful of shavings into the firebox, and added sticks of stove wood. He dropped a match on it and slammed the stove lid back in place. He talked as he filled the coffee pot, dumped a generous helping of coffee beans in a grinder and turned the handle rapidly, then pulled the drawer out and poured the grounds in the pot. He swung around. "What brings you to this neck of the woods?"

Tracker told his story from the beginning, omitting only that Kirby Landers had persuaded Christine to run away with him. He did tell Jess that he knew Christine, had come up to the house to see her when Curly York mentioned her name.

Jess, slicing potatoes into a fry pan, frowned. "It's a rough deal, Sam, mighty rough. How'd you ever come to take on a man like Landers for a partner?" There was a hint of accusation in his voice.

Tracker ignored it but he couldn't ignore the fact that while Jess hadn't changed in physical appearance, he had changed. He shrugged. What the hell. Didn't everyone change from the moment of birth until the day he died? In one way or another, everyone did change. "He seemed to be all right, Jess," Tracker said. He shook his head. "I don't see why you bother to cook when you got a cook for the crew."

Jess frowned. "Curly's the worst damn cook in the world," he grumbled. "He's worse'n me.

Anyway, I get tired of listenin' to the boys all day. I want to get out of their sight after bein' with them all day. It takes a lot outta me tryin' to get a day's work outta them." He slammed the fry pan on the stove and got another from the warmer and began slicing bacon into it. "What're you plannin', Sam?"

"I got to get money for the bank," Tracker said. "It comes due two weeks from tomorrow."

"How much you gotta have?"

"Five thousand. I want to pay it all off."

Jess whistled through his teeth. "That's a sight o' money, Sam."

"Just about what I split with you," Tracker said. "I figured you could make me a loan. I don't want you to give it back."

"From me? Good gawd, Sam." He finished slicing the bacon and slammed the pan on the stove even more violently than the one with the potatoes in it. He pushed a chair around and straddled it and sat there looking at Tracker. "It's been a hell of a year, Sam. Had a big sandy last fall, just when it was supposed to rain. Dust and sand 'til hell wouldn't have it. Lost a lot of stock."

Tracker waited for him to go on, knowing he wasn't finished. He felt a chill in his guts. A sense of desperation seized him.

"This is a funny country, Sam," Hamilton went on. "Three fourths of the people live on the Army. The other fourth lives on the three fourths that's hangin' on the Army. And that damn Army—I still ain't got paid for that last beef shipment to the reservation. Red papers, I mean red tape, papers to fill out, then wait, wait, wait."

"You mean you haven't got it?" Tracker asked mildly.

"That's just about how she lays," Hamilton said uncomfortably, and got up to stir the potatoes and turn the bacon. He tramped to the door. "Watch them spuds and meat. I'm gonna get some bread from Curly." He disappeared through the door.

Tracker sat there with his hands clenched on the table. A rattle against the walls indicated that the wind had risen. He went to the stove, pushed the coffee pot back from the heat, and while he was there poured a cup of coffee. It tasted good. Suddenly, he felt free of the nagging worries that had been dogging him. He was in a hell of a mess any way you looked at it, but he'd been in worse. He had a problem on his hands with the bank, but Bud Sheridan the banker wasn't an unreasonable man. Even if he couldn't raise the money, there were other things to be done. Kirby Landers, for instance, must have disposed of the horses—though if he had, the remount station had forwarded them in a hurry. If he could find Kirby, he might recover some of the money he'd stolen, plus what the horses, if they'd been sold, had brought. What he had to do was find Kirby

Landers, providing his ex-partner hadn't pushed on to California.

Even so, with this thinking behind him, there was another problem—that of Christine. He couldn't ride off and leave her. They'd been something to one another, and he felt responsible for her. He hadn't heard a sound from her since True's gunmen had sent her upstairs. What could he do with her?

Hamilton came stomping in the door with a tray in his hands. He said, "Take these biscuits off the tray, Sam, and I'll take Christine some of Curly's stew."

Tracker removed the biscuits which were on a tin plate and set them on the table. He watched Hamilton move across the room and the look on his face startled Tracker. It was the look of a boy going fishing, or to the circus. It was the eager look of a man about to witness some rare anticipated sight. Hamilton's boots thumped on the stairs and he heard his voice, which rose, and then the tray crashed to the floor.

Hamilton's boots thudded on the stairway and then he burst into the room, his face wild, contorted. "Christine!" he said. "She's gone!"

CHAPTER 6

Hamilton simply stood there with consternation on his face. He held a slip of paper in his hand. Wordlessly, he held it out to Tracker.

Tracker read it.

Dear Sam: I can't face you and I can't stay here. Don't look for me, please. I'll be all right. Christine.

He glanced up at Hamilton.

"What'd you do?" growled Hamilton. "What'd you tell her, Sam? How come she run off when she ain't able to be on her feet?"

"Don't be a fool," Tracker said without trying to curb his sharpness. "She's in better shape than you think, though I grant she shouldn't be out alone. We'll find her."

"What're you standin' there for?" Hamilton's voice was loud, angry. "I'll turn out the boys . . ."

"Jess, Jess," Tracker said, laying his hand on the big man's shoulder. "Take it easy, Jess. She can't be far. And let's not get your crew out. They might not understand."

"Yeah, yeah, guess you're right." Hamilton passed a hand over his face. "Guess I'm kinda spooked, Sam. Don't know what I'm doin'. I'll get the horses." He started for the door.

"Jess, you check outside. She might not be gone yet." He shook his head as Hamilton stumbled through the door at a dead run. This wasn't the cool, calculating Jess Hamilton who'd scouted for Crook. Tracker put the food on the table and by the time he was finished, Hamilton hurried in.

"She's gone, all right. Took the buggy."

"Let's get something to eat before we go," Tracker said. "We'll be damn hungry if we don't."

Hamilton groaned. "How can you think of eatin' when that poor little thing's out there wanderin' around—oh, hell, I guess you're right." He sat at the table and loaded his plate and began wolfing his food.

Tracker poured coffee and sat across the table from Hamilton.

"Curly told me that some of True's men were out here," Hamilton said between mouthfuls.

"Wiltse and Crewe," Tracker said.

Hamilton shook his head in dismay. "Two of the worst," he said. He stopped his jaws for a moment. "Sam, Arnie True's got a horse-stealin' ring set up, the talk goes, in addition to all his other operations."

"Where does James fit in?"

"Leo is Arnie's hound dog. He's not a gunman, but he's more dangerous than Arnie himself. Some folks say Leo's the brains behind Arnie."

"He's afraid of True," Tracker observed.

"Yeah, who ain't? That feller would kill his own

grandmother for the rings on her finger. He's a bad one, Sam, and he's got just about everybody and his brother buffaloed."

"Isn't there any law in Mule Creek?"

"Well, you figger it. Those two you tangled with—they're deputy U. S. Marshals. The sheriff, Ira Hilton, was a good man before Arnie got to him. Circuit judge comes once a month, with the prosecutor, both of 'em beholdin' to Arnie. Sure, there's law, Sam—Arnie True's law."

"Maybe I ought to tuck my tail between my legs and head for the horse ranch," Tracker said. "At least there's half a sack of beans left. And not a gunman in the county."

"Now that you're gone," Hamilton observed. "Come on, Sam, let's go."

When Tracker slipped the two gunbelts over his shoulder, Hamilton stared hard in disbelief. "Hell amighty," he muttered, "you took *their* guns?"

"They still had their saddle guns," Tracker answered. "I got a hunch they'll be waiting somewhere along the road to town. Those kind of men can't afford to let me turn their guns in to a barkeep."

"You told them that?" Hamilton yelled crazily. "You gone completely out of your mind?"

"Listen, Jess, when the cards are down a man does what he has to do. Right now the first item on the tally sheet is Christy. Right?"

Hamilton calmed visibly. "All right, Sam. Let's go."

They were in the saddle and riding through the hot night. The sky was a canopy of velvet studded with brilliant diamond points. The wind was warm, carrying stinging particles of sand.

Suddenly, Tracker turned off the road. Hamilton followed without question. A hundred feet he turned to follow the road at a distance.

"We might run into Wiltse and Crewe if we stay on the road. Let's stay at least this far from it."

"I feel like ridin' hell for leather," Hamilton said.

They rode in silence for half an hour before Hamilton spoke again. "I'm loco about that girl, Sam."

"I could see that," Tracker said dryly.

"What d'you think? That I been eatin' the weed?"

"No, I don't think you're crazy or anything."

"You knew her, Sam. What kind of girl is she?"

"What kind of woman? That's a hard question, Jess. What kind of woman is any female? Some ways they're all alike. . . ."

Jess Hamilton's hand gripped his shoulder and the horses stopped. "Listen, Sam, don't go beatin' around the bush like that. I asked a simple question and I want an answer."

"Jess, you're getting riled for nothing," Tracker murmured. "Christy's a hell of a pretty woman."

"Tell me somethin' I don't know," Jess muttered hoarsely.

"All right, damn it," Tracker's voice rose. "You asked for it and I'll give it to you. We were going to be married, Jess, and she ran off with Kirby Landers. When she got so saddle sore she couldn't ride another step, Kirby left her."

"Oh, hell, oh hell," Jess muttered. "I ain't bawled since I was a kid, Sam, but I feel like doin' it now."

"Maybe it's not her fault," Tracker went on in a more reasonable tone. "She was married to an Army officer, a cavalryman, Major Benton. He got killed in a brush with the Apaches about two years ago. She didn't have any place to go. She'd never known anything but Army. She was lost as a maverick in the badlands. The Army didn't want her. She got to feeling nobody wanted her. I guess maybe I felt sorry for her. Maybe that's why I asked her to marry me. And maybe that's why she ran off with Kirby. That is, she sensed that maybe I pitied her instead of loving her."

"Oh, damn," groaned Hamilton.

"Quit it, Jess."

"I ain't never been around women except dance hall girls," Hamilton said miserably. "I just don't know . . ."

"Shut up!" Tracker said fiercely. "Let's get on with it."

They rode for an hour, just a hundred yards off the road, without hearing anything but the wind and the creak of leather and the soft muffled thud of the horse's hooves in the sand. The lights of Mule Creek appeared in the distance and they halted, listening.

"If Wiltse and Crewe stopped her," Hamilton said, "it's probably here. That clump of pepper trees over there." He pointed to the dark mass a half mile away.

Tracker stepped to the ground. "Hold the horses. I'll Indian up there and have a look."

"Maybe I better go with you."

"Suit yourself," Tracker answered shortly and tied his horse to a mesquite bush. Without waiting for Hamilton he crouched low and went toward the pepper trees.

Hamilton caught up with him. "Wonder why she took the buggy," he muttered.

"Because she's still too sore to ride. She did all her riding in a buggy at Flagstaff. A day in the saddle can ruin a person not used to riding. And she had six days of it."

"You're a hard man, Sam," Hamilton sighed.

"Knock off the talk." Tracker went down on his hands and knees and Hamilton followed.

Working their way in from the town side, they paused often, listening. True's gunmen would no doubt be watching the road from the Rafter H, Tracker thought, and following that the wordless hope: *They'll be looking the other way.*

Tracker stopped and took out his pistol. "You wait here 'til you hear me holler. We'll go in together." He didn't wait for Hamilton's answer but squiggled away.

He came to the road and stopped. He waited there for a long, running moment. He heard nothing but the wind and in the far-off distance a coyote howled. He sucked in his breath and went across the road on his belly.

Across the road he raised to a crouch because the brush grew thickly near the water hole. He went forward almost doubled up, his heart hammering in his chest. He scouted all through the trees and then stood up and walked across the road.

"They're not here, Jess," he called.

Jess Hamilton came into the road and strode toward him, cursing in a strained voice, ending with, "What'll we do, Sam?"

"They're somewhere between here and the ranch, Jess," he said. "Let's get our horses and ride the road back."

"Right out in the road?" Jess asked.

"Hell, yes. We got guns haven't we?"

What Sam Tracker didn't know was that Wiltse and Crewe waylaid him a bare five miles from the Rafter H. They took their horses off to the left side of the wagon road, whereas Tracker and Hamilton went right. The two gunmen staked their horses a good mile away from the road and then returned and took up positions on either side, lying in the sand, concealed by the clumps of bear grass and mesquite and cactus.

They talked now and then, low-voiced, back and forth across the road and most of their talk was of Tracker. Crewe was for killing him outright, but Wiltse, remembering the blow to his throat that had immobilized and humiliated him, wanted Tracker to die slow.

"I'm gonna shoot him in the belly," he said.

"I ain't arguin' with you, Shag," Crewe said. "But he's dangerous. Don't forget it for a minute."

"I—hey, quiet. Here he comes."

But it wasn't Tracker. It was a one-horse outfit, pulling a buggy. The horse shied and snorted when it got between the two men and they saw at the same time that a woman was driving.

Crewe leaped for the horse and pulled its head down and Wiltse grabbed Christine by simply stepping up on the back of the buggy and pinning her arms. The horse lunged and Wiltse swore and half-fell and half-jumped, dragging Christine with him. They fell in the road and Christine began to scream. Wiltse clapped a rough hand over her mouth and lay there, with a wildness beginning to course through him. The feel of a woman's body set him off. He lay there, holding her tight, his breath beginning to quicken while Crewe fought the scared horse.

Crewe got the animal quiet and tied to a bush

and came over quickly. "What the hell?" he said.

"We sure got ourselves a handful," Wiltse said.

"We ain't lookin' for no handful," Crewe said coldly. "Get up from there, Shag. Tracker'll be along any minute."

Wiltse reluctantly rose to his feet, holding his hand over Christine's mouth, his arm clamping her to his body. He removed his hand. "Go ahead and yell," he said. "Ain't nobody gonna hear you."

"Let me go," she said in a voice thinned with fury.

"Hear that, Dub?" chuckled Wiltse. "She wants me to turn her loose."

"Better do it, Shag," Crewe said doubtfully. "We just better put her back in that buggy and let her go."

"I thought you had more backbone than that," complained Wiltse. "I'm gonna keep her for a little bit, Dub."

"The hell you are. Arnie'll have your scalp."

"How's Arnie gonna know?"

"He damn well knows everythin'." He hesitated. "Besides, she's sick."

"She don't look sick to me." He leaned down to peer at Christine's face. "You sick, gal?"

"Please let me go," she said. "I won't tell anyone this happened if you'll let me go. I promise."

Crewe was silent. He'd partnered Shag Wiltse for a number of years and knew of his weakness for women. He had no scruples about Wiltse's intentions. He had no notion of objecting on moral grounds. But they were on a job—a job that had gone wrong. He wanted to right that before doing anything else.

Wiltse said, "Damn me, she's quite a woman, Dub."

Though the night was warm, Christine felt cold and alone. For a long moment she stood there, powerless to do anything except submit to the strong arm that held her tight, locked against a man who smelled of sweat, and horse odors, and bad teeth. She knew she was in dire trouble and there was no help to be expected—unless Sam Tracker—she left the thought suspended.

"Wiltse!" It was a man's voice, edged with savage anger, behind Wiltse and Crewe.

Wiltse had left his rifle on the ground. Crewe swung his saddle gun up and a red flame lashed from the shadows knocking him down. Shag Wiltse swung the girl around and began backing toward his rifle. He felt something slam into his head and he staggered away, releasing Christine, and his mind fuzzed up because he didn't know anyone was in back of him after he turned. He staggered toward his rifle and a dark shape loomed up; the stars exploded in his head.

Christine threw herself into Tracker's arms,

sobbing with relief. Hamilton ejected a shell from his Colt and reloaded. He walked over, knelt beside Crewe.

"This one is dead," he said, and added in a flat voice, "Arnie True'll have us killed for this!"

CHAPTER 7

They rode through the night in silence. The bay gelding was tied behind the buggy. The wind was soft and warm and the daylight blue of the sky was velvet blue dotted with diamonds. The smell of sage and pine from the distant hills mingled.

Tracker broke the silence that had prevailed since he'd helped her into the buggy. "Jess would have liked for you to stay out there." That was putting it mildly, he thought. Jess was frantic for her to return with him but she adamantly refused.

"I didn't want to go back," she said. And then, "I suppose nothing will ever be the same between us."

He didn't deny it and yet there was still a strong attraction to her. She was a lovely, desirable woman. She had a good deal of warm qualities but he knew that her shrewdness broke through, and she used her beauty and womanhood to gain her ends. Looking back on his association with her, he wondered how it was that he hadn't seen a lot of things about her that were now quite plain.

The scene back there at the fight was still fresh in Christine's mind. She recalled, with a sense of shame and embarrassment, that she'd used everything she had to keep from returning to the Rafter H with Jess Hamilton. It was the sensible thing to do but she felt she still had a chance with

Sam Tracker. She'd thrown away one, but she ignored that. It was the future she thought about. She was coldly furious with him for his treatment of her but she didn't let it come through. She tried to stifle the emptiness that drained her, made her feel hollow.

"Will it?" she asked.

"Let's not talk about that," he said. "I want you to put up at the hotel for tonight—what's left of it. Tomorrow or the next day, depending on what I've accomplished, I'll take you out to a friend's house. They're Mexican, but nice people. You can stay there until I get everything under control."

"What's everything?"

"My horses," he said bluntly. "Or the money. The money Landers stole."

"I didn't know he was stealing. He said you and he had split up and the horses belonged to him."

"You didn't know I was trying to catch up?"

She shook her head. "He told me the Apaches were after us."

"They were after me," he said. "If they'd caught me, chances are they'd have caught you. Those horses would have been a big *coup* for them."

She shuddered. "How did I ever get into such a fix?"

"I've wondered too," he said dryly and that ended the conversation.

She was quiet, fuming inwardly. She hadn't handled this right. She tried to remember how she'd worked it when she was Mrs. Stanley Benton, the wife of the major, second in command of Fort Coyotero. The memories were dulled by what had happened in the short span of time since she'd fled with Kirby.

They came into town near midnight and Tracker stopped the buggy in front of the hotel. He went in with Christine and saw her signed in. He stood there until she climbed the stairs to her room and then he went out to the buggy and drove to the livery stable. There was no one around and he turned both animals into a box stall and put grain in the feed box and hay in the manger. He went back outside and pushed the buggy into the shelter, a lean-to on the north side of the big barn.

He turned down the street toward the Bird Cage. He needed a bath and a shave, and the snack he'd eaten at Hamilton's had worn off. He realized he was ravenously hungry. All the eating places were closed, but the free lunch counter in the Bird Cage, if they had one, might still his hunger pains.

He pushed open the door and stepped inside. It was a big room, with a shiny mahogany bar running the full length of one side. A white-shirted, white-aproned bartender with slicked down black hair and a luxuriant black mustache presided at the bar behind which was a huge picture of a reclining woman, her long hair the only covering for her buxom body. There were mirrors on each side of the mural that reflected the tables, the tiny raised platform on which a pianola stood. Back through the archway he caught sight of green-covered card tables, the chuckaluck and blackjack layout and dice table. More men were gambling than drinking. Only three men stood at the bar and they were observing him carefully. One of them wore a star. That'd be Ira Hilton, Tracker guessed.

Tracker walked to the bar and tossed the two gunbelts on the polished counter. The bartender stepped to meet Tracker. The three men looked curiously at the gunbelts and the sheriff moved over to stand beside Tracker.

Tracker spoke to the bartender. "The owner of these guns, one of them anyway, will be calling for it. You mind holding them?"

"Be glad to," the bartender, said, sweeping the gunbelts off the counter and stowing them underneath. "Who'll be calling for them?"

"Shag Wiltse."

The bartender's eyes opened wide. "How'd you get Wiltse's gun?"

"It's a long story."

The sheriff came a step closer. "That other gun belongs to Dub Crewe. What about him?"

"I guess he won't be needing it," Tracker said.

"I'm the sheriff. Maybe you'd better tell me about it."

"I saw your star all right," Tracker said mildly.

"Crewe got himself a case of lead poison. Wiltse only got a gun barrel across his head." He told the sheriff about the events leading up to the meeting with Wiltse and Crewe on the wagon road to the Rafter H. The sheriff listened in stony silence and when Tracker finished he scratched his jaw.

A small crowd had gathered as Tracker narrated the circumstances. All the card players in the back room abandoned their game and listened with intent attention and in complete silence.

"I'd advise you to leave town. You've stirred up quite a ruckus for the short time you've been here." The sheriff was a tall man, with brown hair, and a full mustache, curled at the ends. Sideburns came down to the edge of his jaw and were sharply trimmed. He'd been a lawman most of his life and had developed a sensitivity to trouble. To him, Sam Tracker meant trouble; it was written all over the hard brown face.

"You better wait until you hear it all," Tracker said coolly, "before you start handing out advice."

"What d'you mean by that?"

"I came here chasing a horse thief. I'm sticking around until I find my horses or the thief—or both."

Hilton's face grew hard and his eyes went blank. "I told you to get out of town. You start anything here and I'll lock you up."

Tracker measured Hilton carefully. "Don't try it,

Sheriff. You got a nice, soft job here, and I know you want to keep it."

Hilton's jaw set, and slowly he moved his feet apart. And then he looked into Tracker's eyes and he felt a sudden cold jolt somewhere inside his belly.

Tracker was not running a bluff.

"Don't scratch me, fella," he said softly, but Hilton knew that this was a man he couldn't push. Even if Tracker hadn't brought in Wiltse's and Crewe's guns he'd know it. He felt close to death.

"You try to lock me up," Tracker said implacably, "I'll kill you. I've broken no laws and I won't be put on."

Hilton suddenly found he had nothing to say. With the men looking on, he felt he had to say something; but he knew this man Tracker had gone as far as he would go. Another word and he'd flare up like a roman candle.

"Just watch it," Hilton said, and turned away.

Everyone in the room seemed to breathe out a gusty sigh of relief. Tracker downed a shot of whiskey neat and stalked to the end of the bar where the free lunch was displayed.

He slept in the hayloft of the livery and got out early. He saddled the bay and mounted and ran it out of town, toward the river. He turned downstream as the morning sun put its burning rays on the country. In half an hour he came to the remount station. He stayed on the north side of the corral, away from the stables and the barracks and headquarters building beyond. He sat his horse and gazed at the Army mounts inside the pole enclosure. He didn't spot any T-Bar stock and he started to turn his bay back toward Mule Creek.

"Hey, there!"

He watched the lantern-jawed sergeant come across the corral and step up to the top rail of the fence. He was a sad-faced man in his middle years. "Saw you yesterday," he said. "Lookin' for somethin'?"

"Taking a look at those brands."

"Lose some horses?"

"A few. About seventy-five head."

The sergeant whistled. "That's more than a few. It'd make me foam at the mouth. You figger they'll turn up here?"

"I'm not missing any bets."

"What brand? I might be inclined to keep an eye out for them."

"T-Bar. That's my brand."

"Seems I've seen some up Fort Coyotero way."

"My spread is up there. My name is Tracker."

"Mine's Winslow." He leaned over and offered his hand. "Chances o' you findin' any stole horses here is mighty slim. The major's awful particular about buyin' from strangers."

Tracker didn't particularly believe Winslow, but

he said, "No harm in looking. And it's a short ride out here."

The major appeared on the opposite side of the corral. "Sergeant!"

Winslow said, "Yeah, well," and slipped back into the corral and walked through the horses scattering them. And Tracker turned toward town, riding along the river bank.

He went on toward Mule Creek, riding close to the river, crossing sandbars, splashing through trickles and sloughs. The thickly willowed banks gave an illusion of coolness that wasn't there. He cut across a sandbar and stopped the bay. Another horse stood in a clump of willows, just ahead. Below, close to the murky water, Jean Rainey sat, in the shade of the willows. She was staring out across the wide, sand-colored river. She hadn't heard Tracker's horse moving through the sandbar. He sat his mount, watching her still face, wondering what it was about her that appealed to him and set him to thinking new thoughts. He decided maybe it was the direct, honest look about her. And yet Christine had it too; but she'd fooled him. Jean managed that direct honesty without seeming bold. His horse put its head down and blew noisily, and she looked around quickly and then stood up.

He took off his hat before he stepped down. "Didn't mean to scare you," he said. He wrapped the leathers around a bush and climbed the sloping bank to the willow grove that sheltered them from any except an observer directly across the river. A hot wind fanned them, moving little tendrils of her dark hair over her forehead.

"You didn't," she said.

It seemed to Tracker that a guarded look appeared in her eyes, on her smooth face. She puzzled him, he thought, as he built a smoke, looking at her secretly and liking what he saw.

"Leo told me you're a singer," he said. And then added, "I'd like to hear you sometime."

She smiled faintly and he couldn't tell whether it was a cynical smile or not. Sometimes Christine smiled like that when she thought he was being what she called naïve.

"I did sing," she admitted. "But out here there was—there are other things . . ."

He knew what those other things were. He felt a flash of admiration for her. He wondered how Christine would respond to the situation Jean was in. He knew it'd be different. Jean didn't make excuses for her predicament. She didn't moan about being stranded in a raw and rough western desert town.

"I suppose you'll be leaving here soon's you can," he said.

She glanced at him with surprise. "How'd you know that?"

He moved his big shoulders. "I'd know, even if James hadn't told me."

"You're a friend of Mr. James?"

He shook his head. "I've known him two days," he said. "Two days too many."

She smiled then, a friendly smile that displaced the guarded look. "You don't look like the kind he calls his friends," she said.

Tracker had to laugh at that. They sat in silence for a long moment, looking out across the river. A peacefulness seemed to settle there with them and nothing else was required. It was a feeling as new to Tracker as when he rode his first horse.

"You don't mind me breaking in on your thoughts?"

"I'm glad you came by," she said. "Have you lived here long?"

"Not here. I've a little ranch near Flagstaff. Sure different from all this sand and heat."

"Why, that's not far away," she said wonderingly.

"But it's high. In the mountains you get a cool wind. There's timber and water. Down here it's different. Even the people are different."

"Then why are you here?" she asked.

He talked about himself, then. He told her everything that had happened during the past ten days, even about Christine. She listened with a fascination that widened her eyes, parted her lips. He talked on, and on, and the sun climbed higher and became hotter and they ignored it. At last, it seemed that it was all out of him, all his feelings, all the frustrations, the disappointments, even a part of his dreams.

She was silent for a long time after his voice trailed off and he busied himself with making a cigaret. Then she said, "You must be very careful, my friend." She flushed at the look he gave her, adding, "It wasn't necessary for me to say that, but I had to."

"I'll be careful," he smiled. "Not any other way to play it, I guess." He looked at her. "I'd sure like to know what it is that James wants me to do."

Her reaction was neutral. She shook her head. "I couldn't guess. I don't know much about Mr. James. He's gone most of the time." She eyed him with a slowly growing light of apprehension. "I do know Mr. Wiltse. He's a dangerous man and Mr. True trusts him, has every confidence in him."

"At least we don't have to worry about Crewe," Tracker observed.

She shivered. "He's a bad man, I know, but . . ."

"I'm sorry," Tracker apologized. "I don't mean to joke about death, but I've seen a lot of it out here. As for Crewe being bad, I don't know. I've seen bad men do good. And good men evil. I guess it's the circumstances."

"Yes, I suppose."

"How do True and James get along?"

"They quarrel all the time they are together. No, not exactly quarrel, either. Mr. True would shout and swear and Mr. James would—would cringe.

That's the only word for it. I think he's very much afraid of Mr. True." She rose. "I'll have to go, now. I think I've overstayed my rest period."

She walked to her horse and he put his hand on her arm and helped her mount. The feel of warm flesh made his hand tingle. She sat her horse looking down at him, then she reined about and said, "Good-bye, Sam."

He considered that while he finished his smoke, watching her ride away. He had a nagging notion that she'd wanted to tell him something important and hadn't. Maybe she was afraid.

He mounted and rode upriver and soon came to James's corral.

Leo James sat in the shade of the hayrick, supine with the heat. He held a straw between his teeth and he said, "You didn't lose any time gettin' in trouble, did you?"

"All depends on what you mean by trouble," Tracker observed.

"Yeah, well, Wiltse and Crewe mean trouble aplenty." He looked at Tracker with sleepy eyes. "Didn't connect with your friend, hey?"

Tracker loosened his cinch and stroked the bay's legs. "Wouldn't be here if I had and you know it."

"Then you want t' take on my lil ol' dealy bob?"

"I'll listen," Tracker said. He resisted an inner urge to climb on the bay and head back to Flagstaff. *And then what?* another voice asked. *Go back to a horseless horse ranch? Tell Bud Sheridan, the banker, you haven't any money to pay your note? Sure, Tracker, there's a handful of beans and a half sack of flour in your shack; that'll hold you for a couple of weeks. After that you can trust to luck.* His lip curled at the thought of his recent luck.

"This is a kind of deal I wouldn't even talk about," James said, "if I didn't think you'd take it."

"There's some things I wouldn't do," Tracker pointed out.

"You've killed a man?" James asked. His voice was quietly matter-of-fact.

He shook his head. "In self defense, Leo," he said. "More than once. Never for money, never for any reason except there was no other way."

James spat the straw from his mouth. "You ain't countin' Apaches." His eyes narrowed to thin slits. "Arnie True, he's part Apache, Tracker. Ever' now and then, he puts on a breech clout and takes off in the desert. He goes out there and meets his kin and gawd only knows what they do. I think he's meaner than any o' them bucks he rides with."

"So?" Tracker's heart began to hammer. This Leo James wasn't just the soft, fat coyote he pretended to be. Tracker remembered Maria's warning, and Jean Rainey's admonition to be careful. He shrugged.

"You notice Arnie's eyes, Tracker? It wouldn't make no difference to Arnie if he killed you or not. You get in his way, he'd kill you."

Tracker said, "I'm not in his way. I've never hired to kill and I wouldn't."

James got to his feet. "I'm satisfied," he said. "Now that's what I wanted to know. I'm not like Arnie. I don't want no hired killer working for me. You and me, we can do business."

Tracker brought out his tobacco sack, thinking about what James had said, which wasn't much. It rang about as true as a lead dollar. He waited for James to go on.

"I just wanted to make sure you wouldn't put a bullet in Arnie," James said. "There's some talk goin' around that you're hell on Apaches. I wouldn't want Arnie put out o' the way like a wild Apache. Arnie's real smart an' I need him."

"I think he's real smart," Tracker agreed.

"Now here's what I want. There's a paperboard box in Arnie's desk. It belongs to me. It's about eighteen inches long and ten inches wide and, say, maybe six inches deep. It's all tied up with a piece o' grass rope. You get if for me and I'll pay you good."

"What is good?" Tracker asked. His fingers were steady as he rolled a cigaret but his thoughts were racing.

"Well, you lost seventy head to Landers," James said. "At a hundred a head that'd be seven thousand. I'll give you half that for gettin' me that lil ol' box in Arnie's desk."

"Seventy-five head," Tracker said, his eyes suddenly cold and expressionless.

"Yeah, but five—well, how about it?" James moved uneasily and the sweat on his face suddenly seemed heavier. "You want it or dontcha?"

"Sure, I'll take it," Tracker said. "Though I'm wondering why you don't take it yourself?"

"Well, me, I'm gonna have Arnie busy so's to give you a chance to get it."

Tracker dropped his cigaret in the sand and stepped on it. "What time you got it planned for, Leo?"

James sighed deeply, as though relieved. "Ten o'clock tonight."

"No, not tonight. How about tomorrow night?"

"If that's the best you can do. Tomorrow night. Ten o'clock sharp. I'll be busy with Arnie up front, keepin' him occupied. Go down the alley at ten sharp. Right through the door, the way you and me went. Get it out o' his desk and come back here to the corral. I'll pay you cash, and you can make tracks out o' here."

"Sounds like it's all planned out. You really got it figured."

"Yeah. It ain't five thousand like you wanted. But it's a long way toward it, Tracker."

"Right." Tracker turned and stepped up in the

saddle as a small herd of horses came swinging in toward the corral. He watched James run and open the corral gate and stand there to keep the horses inside from escaping. Tracker continued to sit his horse and watch as the herd swept into the corral. The two wranglers, sweaty and dust-stained, pulled up, casting quick, shifty glances at him, while James closed the corral gate.

Tracker reined the bay around and started walking him toward town. The horses just hazed into the corral bore the Lazy A brand, that of Frank Cady; the horses Tracker and James had spooked the night before last, on the road to Mule Creek.

CHAPTER 8

Tracker walked his horse into town. He was worried about Cady and his daughter Pat. The Lazy A horses just turned into James's corral could mean big trouble for Cady. Moreover, the revealing talk Leo James had made filled him with an eagerness akin to that he'd experienced when Landers waylaid him. He cautioned himself to avoid letting his eagerness override his caution. Sam Tracker was positive he hadn't told James how many head of horses he'd lost. It was true that Kirby had taken seventy-five head, but five of those horses were mares and wouldn't be acceptable to the Army. And James had very nearly divulged even that bit of information.

Tracker gave the bay to the liveryman and talked with the man about Jess Hamilton's horse and buggy, which Tracker had left there the night before.

"I may be using the rig again," Tracker said. "Tell that to Jess if he shows up before I do."

The liveryman promised and Tracker went on down the high boardwalk to the general merchandise store where he bought shirt, pants, underwear, and socks. From there he went to a barber shop across the street, run by a friendly barber from Mississippi. The sign over the mirror said FREE HAIRCUTS TO ALL MISSISSIPPIANS. FROM THERE MYSELF.

He had a hot bath in a big tin tub, relaxing in the warm water, and listening to the idle chatter in the barber shop on the other side of the partition. He examined his furrowed rib. The herbs Maria had put on the wound had dried out. He removed bits of dried leaves, roots, and bark, and his side looked clean, the flesh pink and healthy; it didn't pain him at all.

After a good soaking, he scrubbed with soap and water and rinsed off. He got out of the tub and dried on the rough towel and dressed in his stiff new clothes. He rolled his dirty clothes in a small bundle and went out into the shop and climbed into the chair.

"I'll collect that free haircut," he said. "I originally come from Guntown, Mississippi."

The barber was tall and thin with a long, thin neck and deep-sunk brown eyes. "Sho' 'nuff," he said, beaming. "Well, by doggies, I'm from Tupelo, we was practically neighbors. How long you been gone?" He stuck out his hand. "I'm Pete Randle."

"Sam Tracker." Tracker shook hands with Randle. "I left there when I was about ten or eleven. My folks went to Texas and got scalped by Comanches."

"Aw, shoot, that's awful. I lived in Tupelo 'til about fo'-five years ago." He tapped his chest. "Doc told me to get outta that damp climate."

"You went from the dampest to the driest."

"And that's a fact," Randle declared. He went to work on Tracker, cutting his hair, shaving him, and even giving his hair a liberal dose of some sweet-smelling hair tonic, talking a blue streak all the time. He regretfully watched Tracker depart, calling after him to come again.

Tracker felt good as he tramped over to the hotel. He climbed the stairs and knocked on Christine's door. She opened it at once, as though she'd been waiting. When she saw him, her eyes filled with tears and she threw her arms around his neck and pressed herself to him.

"I thought you'd gone and left me alone," she sobbed.

His heart went out to her. He patted her shoulder, comforted her, telling her he was thoughtless for not being there when she awakened, feeling that he was back in the other days, when nothing but warmth had been between them. "I had a few things to do," he explained.

She dried her eyes, smiling mistily at him. "I'm such a sissy, the major always told me."

"There's no need to apologize," he said.

As she looked at him her eyes filled with tears again. "Damn," she said through clenched teeth. "If I were a man. . . ."

"A lot of men would be real unhappy," he said.

She didn't look at him. "Sam, I've got to tell you."

Something in her voice caused him to look at her and he felt an expectant excitement fill him. "What?"

Her voice was muffled. "Kirby Landers. He's here—in this hotel." She turned to face him. "He's in a room right down the hall, third door right."

The look in his eyes scared her but he wheeled and walked out the door and down the hallway, not even knowing she followed. He stopped in front of the door, hearing footsteps inside, a man moving around.

He gripped the knob and turned it slowly and pushed easy. The door was locked. He backed away and plunged against it, knocking it loose from the flimsy catch, hurtling on into the room.

A heavy-shouldered man turned to stare. He was stripped to the waist, and he was washing in a white porcelain bowl on a washstand. His gunbelt hung on a brass knob of the bedstead. The man froze, his mouth open, his breath coming in little gasps that were plainly audible.

"Hello, Kirby," Tracker said in a quiet voice. "Where's my money and my horses?"

Kirby Landers looked at the gun on the bedstead with longing eyes. He looked at Tracker and a twisted grimace that might have been a smile was on his face. "You ain't got a thing to worry about, Sam," he said smoothly. He hung up the towel and his hand dropped to the water pitcher. He picked it up and flung it in one smooth motion, and dove for Tracker.

Tracker stepped aside, and the water pitcher crashed against the wall and shattered, the pieces flying around the room. Tracker brought his boot up and met Kirby's flying tackle. Kirby thudded into the wall. He got to his hands and knees, his head hanging, blood from his nose and mouth dripping to the floor. He shook his head dazedly.

Flaming rage invaded Tracker. He stepped forward and savagely grabbed a handful of Kirby's black hair. He lifted the bigger man to his feet and slammed his fist into Kirby's handsome face, eliciting a spray of blood. Kirby whined deep in his throat and flailed his arms ineffectively at Tracker. Tracker slapped him repeatedly, his palm cracking against Kirby's flesh.

"Where's my money and horses?" Tracker asked again in an even cold tone.

"Let me go, Sam," Kirby gasped through bloody lips. "Let me go and I'll tell you!"

Tracker gave him a shove and Kirby lunged toward the bed. He got his hands on the gun before Tracker reached him. Kirby whirled with the gun in both hands, his eyes wild with rage. He triggered a shot that tugged at Tracker's shirt. The gun went off again as Tracker hit him with both hands clasped together, knocking him across the bed. Tracker leaped after him and the bed collapsed with a crash that shook the building.

Footsteps thudded on the stairway as Kirby tried to jam his thumbs in Tracker's eyes. Tracker jerked his head away and then bit down viciously, tasting blood as Kirby yelled and jerked his hand away. Tracker hammered Kirby's head with his hard fists and then grabbed a handful of hair and slammed his head against the floor.

Tracker staggered to his feet as Sheriff Ira Hilton plunged into the room, a gun in his hand. The frightened face of the hotel clerk peered over Hilton's shoulder.

Still dazed from the blow Kirby had hit him with the gun, Tracker grinned drunkenly at the sheriff. "Glad you showed up," he said. "Guess maybe I'd of killed him if you hadn't."

Kirby Landers stirred on the floor and Tracker stepped over and pulled him up and pushed him into a chair. "Want to tell me where my horses are, Kirby?" he asked in an almost gentle voice.

The sheriff moved close with his gun pointed at Tracker. "Don't make me no trouble," he warned. He reached out gingerly, got Tracker's gun and shoved it in his belt, motioning with his own gun. "Get goin', fella. I'll tell you where to turn and when to stop."

"Where you taking me, Sheriff?"

"To jail, o' course. Ain't you been asking for it?"

"You're making a mistake, Hilton."

"I've made quite a few, Tracker. One more ain't gonna make much difference."

At the door Tracker had a glimpse of Christine sponging Kirby's battered face. He sighed, trying to ignore the sick feeling that permeated his stomach.

The crowd fell back as Tracker came through the door, followed at a respectable distance by the sheriff. He recognized Pete Randle, the barber, and Jean Rainey among them.

With the sheriff giving monosyllabic directions, Tracker soon arrived at the jail and was locked up, in the single cell. There were no other prisoners. The sheriff slapped the ring of keys on a nail on the wall and said, "There," with satisfaction in his voice.

Tracker leaned against the bars in the stifling hot jail and said, "I guess you feel real proud of yourself, Hilton."

Ira Hilton sat at his battered desk and leaned back in the creaky swivel chair. "Not particularly," he said. "You been trying to break into my jail ever since you got to Mule Creek. Now you ought t' be happy."

"You heard what I asked Landers, didn't you?"

"You mean Mr. Andrews? That fella you slugged is Jason Andrews."

"Maybe that's how you know him. His name is Kirby Landers." He looked sharply at the sheriff but Hilton kept his head turned. "And to think Jess

Hamilton said you was a good sheriff once upon a time."

The sheriff glanced at him for the first time. "You know Jess?"

"Yes. The way Jess told it, you were a good man until Arnie True got his hooks into you."

"That's rubbish," Hilton said flatly. "Jess is still pretty sore at me for not runnin' a squatter off his place a couple years back. That's his trouble." He sounded angry.

"Well, no matter, I believe *him*," Tracker said. "And others do too. I came here looking for a man that stole five thousand of my dollars and seventy-five of my horses. I found him and you arrest *me*. Those simple facts back up what Jess Hamilton told me about you."

"You're a fool, Tracker," Hilton said indecisively.

"When are you going to let me out of here?"

"I dunno. The circuit judge just left. Won't be back for nearly a month."

"You mean you're going to keep me locked up until then?"

"I guess it boils down to that," Hilton said. He abruptly got up and walked to the door. "I'll see you come suppertime." He stepped through the door and Tracker heard his boots clamping down the boardwalk.

He was midway through a cigaret when a light step sounded outside and Jean Rainey came through the door. She looked around the room uncertainly and then said, "The sheriff isn't here."

"He said he'd see me at supper," Tracker said sourly.

She came across the room and stood before the barred door. "It's just as well. I wanted to tell you I'm sorry."

"Thanks," he said. "I'm glad you came. You know Jason Andrews?"

She looked startled and then nodded. "Yes, I know him."

"He's the man who stole my money and horses. I told you about it."

Her eyes lowered and her fingers were suddenly busy with the folds of her dress. "He—he's a thief?"

Tracker nodded. "His real name is Kirby Landers. He was my partner. I told you about it."

"Yes," she said. "You told me, Mr. Tracker."

"I tried to recover my property. You saw what happened. I wish you'd call me Sam." He half smiled. "What's Landers up to?"

She looked directly at him then and he felt almost helplessly lost in the dark depths of her eyes. "He's in trouble, Sam. He's been trying to sell the horses to the Army. Major O'Donnel won't buy them. Mr. True has some sort of arrangement with the major, and Landers has been trying to get True to handle the sale for him."

"I see," Tracker said thoughtfully. "Someone

comes along with horses and tries to sell them and the Army turns them down. Then True buys the horses and resells them to the Army. Is that how it works?"

"That's how," she said, nodding.

"I understand," Tracker said bitterly. "When I was a kid, I remember this planter's store. My father was a sharecropper and year after year he traded at the farm store. He always ended up owing money to the man he worked for. He managed somehow to get a little ahead and tried trading somewhere else. He found he couldn't buy. That's when we moved to Texas."

"Oh, Sam!" She was silent for a moment and then said, "What I really came for was to see if I could help you in any way."

"I've got to write some letters," he said. "I need paper and envelopes."

"You tell me what to say and I'll write the letter and see it's mailed."

"I want to let my banker know I intend to come back," Tracker said, and smilingly added, "someday. And I want to write the Territorial governor and tell him about this mess here and ask for his help."

"Do you think the governor will help?"

Tracker shook his head. "That I can't tell. But at least I'll have a clear conscience."

"A clear conscience?"

"Sure. What I'm going to do is let them know.

What they do after that is up to them as men with a public trust. And when the dust starts boiling up here, they'll know why."

"I think I can write your letters," she said, smiling at him, "without any notes or anything else. I know what you want to say."

He reached through the bars and touched her hand. "Thanks," he said. "There's one other letter to write, too."

She looked at him questioningly.

"The commanding officer at Fort Coyotero. Just tell him there's some monkey business going on at the Mule Creek Remount Station that should be looked into by the Inspector General."

"An honest Inspector General," she said, still smiling.

He nodded. "Yeah, an honest one." He watched her as she walked across the room through the open door.

CHAPTER 9

In the late afternoon the wind rose, brushing sand against the adobe walls of the jail. The town stirred out of its midday lethargy. Tracker could hear voices drifting down the alley which opened on the jail. He couldn't make out what was being said, only the sound of men talking. A wagon creaked slowly down the alley, the trace chains jangling. A man cursed cheerfully as a wagon wheel scraped against the adobe wall.

Time went slowly and the locked-in feeling built an urgency inside him. He walked to the one small barred window that was over his head. He reached up and gripped the iron bars. They were rigidly set in adobe. He walked back and forth on the dirt floor, from the bars to the end of the wall. He moved back and forth to keep from being consumed by his frustration. *What a hell of a way to end up,* he thought bitterly.

A lizard ran along the window ledge and stopped, looking at him with unblinking eyes. Tracker moved his hand and the lizard scurried away. A fly buzzed lazily through the window and droned across the cell and into the sheriff's office. Tracker felt like shouting, and to ease the desire he walked up and down the cell again. He halted by the bars when the outside door opened and the sheriff came in carrying a tray of food.

Hilton let the door remain open. He walked across the office and set the tray on a chair beside the cell door. He said, "Howdy. Brought you supper." He walked to the wall and got the keys and came back and unlocked the door. He looked at Tracker. "Move to your bunk and sit down."

Tracker's jaw muscles tightened and his face darkened; but he walked to the bunk and sat down. The sheriff opened the door and shoved the chair and tray inside the cell, closed and locked the door. He went over and hung the keys back on the nail and went to his desk and slumped in his chair. "Better eat while it's hot," he advised.

Tracker pulled the chair over to his bunk and sat on the bunk and picked up the knife and fork. The food was from the Chinaman's restaurant and the Mexican cook didn't know how to fry a steak. It was leathery and the potatoes were soggy. Instead of bread there was tortillas. He grunted and began eating silently.

Hilton sucked his teeth and ran his tongue around his gums. "You sure stirred up a hornet's nest," he said finally.

Tracker kept on eating and didn't answer the charge. Being sheriff in a hardcase town wasn't the easiest job in the country, and Tracker had no intention of trying to make it any easier.

"Shag Wiltse's in town making war talk."

He would be doing that, Tracker thought

morosely, chewing on the leathery steak. He glanced up at the small barred window. A man could see in from saddle height outside. And shoot in. Or a man could shoot through the open outside door, through the sheriff's office and into the cell. But a man like Shag Wiltse wouldn't get any fun out of cold turkey shooting like that. Wiltse wouldn't shoot him in jail. Tracker recognized the breed Wiltse belonged to at once—the hired fighting man, dangerous as a wounded lion, skilled with guns, the tools of his trade. Wiltse and Crewe had seen the wars together and obviously were close; or had been. Wiltse would avenge Crewe's death, but he wouldn't come in here and shoot Tracker—unless Tracker was in for a long, long time and Wiltse got impatient. He dismissed Wiltse from his mind.

"You hear what I'm tellin' you?" Ira Hilton asked in a sharp, angry voice.

"I hear," Tracker speared the last piece of boot heel meat and ground it between his teeth. "That steak come off a steer near as old as I am," he observed.

Hilton swore in a soft, perplexed voice. "Maybe I ought to take you to Phoenix for protection."

"You going to send Wiltse along as an armed escort?"

"You shut up that kind of talk, Tracker," Hilton said angrily. "I'm doin' the best I know how. Shag'll kill you he gets a chance. I know him.

Only thing botherin' me is how to get you out o' town without anybody knowin'."

"The way Arnie True operates, that'd be impossible," Tracker said.

Ira Hilton felt irritated and hemmed in. When he had taken this job he'd been proud to wear the badge, and he was beholden to no man. But then Arnie True had come along and quickly rose to be the big man in the country. It was true that he'd pulled in his horns and the knowledge didn't make him feel good. Worse, this man Tracker looked and acted like a man who wouldn't be trifled with. Tracker was a hard man, a fighter, and Hilton respected these qualities because he had them in some measure himself.

Tracker rose and came to the bars and stared out at Ira Hilton. "Sheriff, you're nearly in as big a mess as I am. And I got no sympathy for you. You're bringing it on yourself."

"What d'you mean by that?"

"I think you know what I mean," Tracker said quietly.

Hilton impatiently got out of his chair and strode to the bars. "You think you know so damn much," he grated. "I ought to just forget about you, Tracker. If Wiltse plugs you that'll be your tough luck."

"He won't," Tracker said indifferently. "Not unless he thinks I'm going to be locked up for a long time."

"Shag's not a patient man," Hilton said impatiently. "Shove that chair over and let me get the tray back to the Chinaman's." He felt as though he had to be doing something. Carrying a tray back to the restaurant wasn't much, but it did keep him moving and that way he wouldn't have to think too much. He watched as Tracker shoved the chair to the door and returned to the bunk and sat down. Hilton opened the door, pulled the chair out and closed and locked the cell door but he didn't leave at once. He stood there looking at Tracker, a perplexed frown on his face. Tracker's words had the effect of deepening his worry. "Just what d'you mean, I'm in as much trouble as you?"

Tracker got to his feet and tramped over to the cell door. "There's a hell of a lot going on in this town," he said, "that don't look good and don't smell good. I think you know damn well what it is and you refuse to recognize it. Maybe one man can't fight it but you sure as hell could let someone in authority know about it."

"Let someone know I can't handle a two-bit sheriff's job?"

"It might have started out a two-bit job," Tracker said evenly. "It's not two-bit any longer."

The door opened and the sheriff whirled and dropped his hand to his gun. He relaxed as Jess Hamilton and Pete Randle, the barber, came into the room.

Jess said, "What you got him locked up for?"

"Yeah, wha' fo' you got him locked up?" Pete Randle seconded accusingly. He looked apologetically at Tracker. "We sho' 'nuff ain't much on hospitality, suh. Not lak down in ol' Missy."

Ira Hilton opened his mouth and then shut it. He straightened up. "I locked him up for near killin' a man," he said with some dignity.

"That ain't like I heard it," Jess Hamilton said angrily. "He was tryin' to get back what was his'n."

"An' that's the Lawd's troof," amended Pete Randle.

Hilton looked from one to the other and his dilemma grew in proportion to the influence Jess Hamilton had in the county. Ira Hilton respected money and power, even more than he respected a hard and dangerous fighter, because the two of them together represented something he'd never had. Jess Hamilton had money; he had influence in Phoenix, and with the honest people in and around Mule Creek. Pete Randle was an ignorant southern Negro, but a lot of people stopped in his shop. Moreover, Randle had a knack of talking that a lot of barbers seemed to have. A man in a barber chair was just about helpless. He had to listen. And whatever Pete Randle chose to tell them, some of it would stick.

"I been thinkin' about it," Hilton said slowly, judiciously, choosing his words with care so a man wouldn't get the idea he was backing down. "I don't think he's safe in my jail, not with Shag Wiltse runnin' loose."

"Then let him go," Jess Hamilton said. "I've known him a good many years and there's not a straighter man living."

"Thanks, Jess," Tracker said in an amused voice.

"Now, you quit spurrin' me," Hilton said, "I'm doin' the best I can." He turned from Jess to Tracker and said, "Listen, if I turn you loose, will you get out of town?"

"That's a fair offer," Jess said. "What about it, Sam?"

"I don't reckon that's the polite way o' doin' it," Pete Randle objected.

"You shut up, Pete," Jess said.

"Now, listen, Mr. Hamilton," Pete Randle said, his sunken cheeks puffing out. "I got a lot o' respect fo' you, suh, but . . ."

"Hold it, Pete," Tracker interposed. "That isn't necessary." He looked at Hilton. "I won't leave town without my money and horses."

Hilton shrugged. "It's out o' my hands, then. I can't let you loose to go bear huntin', Tracker."

"You harbor all thieves?" Tracker asked scornfully, "or just them that Arnie True picks out?"

"You shut that kind of talk," Hilton said angrily. "I ain't gonna put up with it!"

"Sam, Sam," Jess chided. "Why don't you take him up on it? Like I said, I haven't got that five thousand you wanted, but I could stretch a point and make it two thousand. That'd tide you over until you get on your feet again."

"Jess, you and I put in a lot of hard miles," Tracker said, smiling. "I figured I knew you as well as I know myself and I sort of expected you to know me as well. I can see you don't know me at all."

"That spells out you're refusin'?" Jess asked.

"It does."

Jess wheeled. "I can't make up his mind for him, Ira. He's got to do that himself." He strode to the door and yanked it open. He went out, followed by Pete Randle.

"You're kind of foolish," Ira Hilton said.

"Maybe. Just put yourself in my shoes for a minute."

"That's hard to do."

"Not so much so. I take it you're an honest lawman—or want to be. Think of yourself as owner of a prosperin' ranch. Your partner runs out on you with four years' work and all the money. You track him down and he nearly kills you. He does kill your horse. Then when you catch up with him, what're you going to do? Just say politely, 'Give me back my horses and money,' or do you beat it out of him?"

"Listen, Tracker," Hilton said desperately, "I

know you got cause. I gave you a chance to get out o' jail, get out o' town, and you turned me down. What else can I do?"

"Don't shout," Tracker said calmly. "I'm right here. What else can you do? There's one hell of a lot you can do—if you're man enough to do it." He could sense Hilton's indecision and it gave rise to an eagerness that he realized could be dangerous; he kept reminding himself not to say too much.

Hilton's mouth whitened but he didn't shout. He said quietly, "You'd better talk plainer than that, Tracker."

Tracker put his boot on an iron strap supporting the vertical bars of his cell. He said, "All hell's going to break loose in this town when the governor gets my letter, Hilton."

Hilton stared at him. "You wrote to the governor?"

Tracker nodded. "I give him all the facts, Sheriff, the way I see them. A man who runs the county for his own thieving good. I mean Arnie True. He's got the Army purchasing agent here in his pocket. He deals in stolen horses."

"You can't prove that," Hilton said flatly.

"The hell I can't. I was talking to Leo James today. While I was there, a bunch of Lazy A branded horses were driven into Leo's corral. Know who owned those horses a couple of days ago? A rancher named Frank Cady from Salt

Valley. Cady's probably dead. He had a girl with him, a young girl, his daughter Pat. What happened to her?"

"I don't know nothin' about no Frank Cady," Hilton said.

"Well, I do and I'm telling you. And something else, Sheriff. Leo James made me an offer today, too. Thirty-five hundred dollars if I stole a box out of Arnie True's desk. He said it belonged to him but he couldn't get it without help. Know what I think he's cooking up?"

"How would I know?" Hilton growled irritably. He wasn't a smart man, and he had the advantage of knowing it. He followed things slowly and it bothered him to have too many things to think about.

"Leo and Arnie don't get along. Everybody knows that. I think Leo is going to kill Arnie and try to pin the murder on me. That's why he wanted me to get that box for him. When I picked it up, one of his buddies would be waiting. If I was fool enough to go through with it, Arnie would be dead when I went for that box. If there is a box there."

"Sounds like a lot of horse manure to me," Hilton said.

"Well, let's give it a try. I'm not supposed to get that paperboard box until tomorrow night. Suppose you let me out. I'll stay out of Wiltse's way and I won't go after Kirby until this proves out. What do you say?"

Darkness had come down like a shadow as they talked. Tracker couldn't see Hilton's face but he knew the man was thinking hard. Hilton walked to the desk and scratched a match and lighted the coal oil lamp. He turned up the wick and wheeled to Tracker, shaking out the match. "I want to let you go," he said in a troubled voice, "but . . ." He stopped and was silent, thinking hard thoughts.

Tracker felt a thrill of victory and pressed ahead. "You can make a big name for yourself. Instead of waiting for the governor to take action, you clean it up yourself. That'd be a lot of feathers in your war-bonnet, Sheriff."

Hilton jangled the keys indecisively and then he straightened up. "All right, Tracker," he said, striding to the cell door. "I'll be bettin' my star that you're right." He unlocked the door and stood back.

A voice spoke from the outside door as Tracker stepped out of the cell. "Stand where you are, Ira." Shag Wiltse's voice was dangerous. "You won't get hurt if you do."

Even though the gun was slanting at Hilton's feet he made a fast play for the gun on his belt. He never cleared leather. Wiltse's bullet caught him and flung him against the bars.

Tracker made a bounding leap through the window as another of Wiltse's bullets knocked the heel off his boot.

CHAPTER 10

Tracker hit the sand of the alley, his hands breaking his fall. His chest thumped solidly, driving the breath from him momentarily. He felt the sting of his hands where they contacted the ground. He didn't stop moving, but rolled effortlessly to his feet and ran close to the side of the building, toward the back of the alley. He had a glimpse of Wiltse leaning from the window. The flame lanced at him and he heard the sound of the bullet; then he was around the corner of the building, the town on his left, the desert on his right.

He heard a shout in the street and yet he slowed, then stopped. He was in a dangerous spot. He didn't know how many men would be turned out looking for him but he thought there would be quite a few; perhaps twenty. Without a horse he couldn't go far in the desert.

He had to stay in town; but where?

He began walking, hugging the shadows of the rear of the buildings facing the main street. He went quickly across another alley and saw that he was in back of the hotel. He thought then of Jean Rainey. She lived in the hotel. She'd hide him for a time, perhaps find a gun and horse for him. Trouble was, he didn't know which room was the one she occupied.

But there was someone in the hotel who would know—Christine. And he knew her room number—just a few doors down from where he'd had his bitter fight with Kirby Landers.

He turned, crossed the porch, opened the door and stepped inside, into the darkness. From where he stood, he could see a portion of the lobby. He couldn't walk up the stairs leading off the lobby. There must be stairs at the back for patrons using the outhouse. He moved along the wall, feeling his way and then his feet encountered stairs. He went quietly up the stairs, walking close to the wall so the treads wouldn't creak. He heard hasty footsteps on the boardwalk outside, and then excited voices in the lobby of the hotel.

A search party was gathering.

He reached the top of the stairs and then hastily backed down as someone came tramping along the hallway. If the man was going outside, Sam Tracker would have to retreat all the way down, raising his chance of exposure. He stood there and sighed with relief when the footsteps halted before a door. The metallic click of a key reached him. The door opened and the man went into the room, closing the door behind him.

Tracker went up the stairs again without making a sound.

He walked on the tip of his boots down the hallway and stopped in front of the door to Christine's room. He put his head against the door and could hear nothing. He tried the knob. The door was locked.

Looking up and down the hall, he tapped gently with one knuckle, his head close to the door. He didn't get any response so he tapped again, a bit harder.

Christine answered, "Who is it?"

Damn, he thought, *why doesn't she simply answer by opening the door.* He put his mouth close to the wood and murmured, "Let me in, Christy."

He thought he heard a gasp and then the sound of the latch being pulled back made a welcome noise. The door swung open.

She was wearing a kimono and her hair was covered with a scarf. She looked up at him, wide-eyed, frightened. He stepped into the room and pushed the door shut.

Still staring at him, her hands clutching the kimono to her, her lips parted as she said, "Sam, Sam, you—you . . ." then stopped speaking and walked to a chair and sat down. She was pale.

"What's the matter?" he asked, in a low voice, and came to stand beside her.

"They—they say you killed the sheriff."

"They lie," Tracker said flatly. "Wiltse killed him." He dropped to one knee beside her chair. "Jean Rainey. What room is she in?"

He had to repeat the question. She looked at him with glazed, unseeing eyes. "Sam, I don't know—

yes, I do. I saw her coming out of the room at the end of the hall."

Damn, Tracker thought again. Everything seemed to be working against him. That was the room the man in the hallway had gone into. Had used a key. He felt the quickened beat of his heart, a sickness down in his gut. Were all women like this one? he wondered. But no! There was still another room at the end of the hall, on the opposite side. That must be Jean's room. He said, "I want you to walk down there and tell her to step in here for a minute. Don't tell her I'm here. Understand?"

She still had that vacant look in her eyes. She stared at him as though he were a stranger. He shook her lightly and she looked at him again with clearing eyes. "Why, Sam? Why do you want her to come here?"

"I must talk to her. Go get her. And hurry. I may not have much time."

She rose and went to the door. She turned once and looked at him; then she went out and pulled the door shut.

Tracker waited. He considered the town, remembering it as well as he could from his view of it from a distance, and from his walking and riding through and around it. The town lay a quarter-mile from the river, on a slight rise, its position determined by the adequate water supply, a cold spring that bubbled from the ground here, a natural artesian well. The town had one main street, flanked with the business houses of the merchants, artisans, and professional men. He was right in the middle, the hotel being centrally located. A group of men could go through this town, he thought, building by building, room by room, before the night was over.

He expected them to do exactly that.

What, then, would they expect him to do?

They would foresee that he'd try to get his horse. That meant one or two men would have the bay staked out, watching, ready for him if he should appear. Also, they'd be expecting him to hide out in town. Already, he guessed that a group of searchers were methodically turning the town upside down. They would not expect him to hide out in the desert; they knew they'd have nothing to fear there. A man alone in the desert, without water, horse or gun, would be near helpless and a dead man in no time at all.

So True and his men would concentrate on the town.

He came to his feet as the door opened and Christine came in and swiftly closed it. She faced him. "She's not there. She hasn't been in her room all day, or night."

He wondered at the meaning of that. "How do you know?"

"I asked." She looked at the floor. "Mr. Tabor, a mining man from Quartz Town is across the hall.

131

He says he's been watching for her. Wanted her to have dinner with him. When she didn't come in at the usual time he went over to True's office. She wasn't there either."

Tracker scrubbed his jaw with a knuckled hand, scowling. This didn't sound good to him. He wondered if, by any chance, True had caught Jean writing those letters. He chuckled, dismissing it as too fantastic. But it was a disquieting thought.

"Where did Kirby go?"

She shook her head. "I don't know. You beat him so badly—I went for a doctor. When I came back he was gone. I don't know where."

"I've got to have a gun," he said. "And my horse. How'm I going to get them?"

"Is that why you wanted to see her?" Christine asked.

He waited a moment and then shrugged, nodding.

"Why didn't you ask me first?" she asked with a hurt little laugh. "Why didn't you, Sam?"

He didn't answer at once because he was searching his mind for his own answer. Why had he thought of Jean instead of Christine? Christine had been a last resort, only a way to find Jean. Yet, a short month ago he'd been very close to this woman, as close as a man and woman can be without actually becoming man and wife. He shrugged again and said, "I thought she could move around without arousing attention."

"That's a lie," Christine said. She straightened and walked up to him. "But I've asked for this treatment, lying to you, running away. I want to help now, Sam. I want you to hide out here. They're searching the town but they won't search my room. I won't let them."

"I can't hole up. I've got to get a horse and gun and get out. Every minute counts."

"And I don't believe you killed the sheriff, either."

A sudden, sickening truth streaked through him. He looked at her with hard, bright eyes, trying to pierce the mask that had been erected since she left the room. She was trying too hard to keep him there. He moved casually to the door and slipped the latch. He stood with his face to the door, standing motionless, listening.

She crossed the room to him. "Why did you bolt the door?"

"Be quiet. I'm listening."

"You've nothing to worry about . . ."

He whirled and crossed the room and raised the window as the doorknob rattled. He thrust a leg through the window and bent his shoulder. He looked at her, saw the agony in her face and knew she'd tried to betray him. The door shook against the impact of a shoulder. Tracker poised on the window ledge and leaped through the air.

He landed on the edge of the adjoining building, teetered there for a moment, regained his balance and jumped down to the roof. A dark shape rose out of the night and Tracker lunged ahead, his booted feet propelling him forward like a catapult. His head took the man in midsection and the two of them crashed to the roof with a jarring thump. Tracker's hand held the gun hand of the struggling man and his knee came up in violent contact with the man's groin. There was an explosive scream and Tracker twisted the gun out of the suddenly weak fingers and streaked on across the roof. He leaped across to the adjoining building and ran across that, dropped to a one-story roof, crossed it, and went over the edge, hanging by his fingertips and then dropping to the ground.

He crouched in the dark alley, listening to the wild shouts that went up and down the street. Voices called back and forth and some of them were getting close. . . .

Tracker was on the back side of the buildings again, moving quietly, stopping often to listen. Once he crouched in a darkened doorway as a man came to a back door and tossed out a pan of water. He caught a glimpse of the sunken-faced barber, Pete Randle. A moment later he tapped on the door, calling softly, "Pete, Pete!"

Randle called, "Who is it?"

"Tracker, Pete. Mississippi. I want to hole up for a while."

Pete Randle opened the door and Tracker

walked in quickly and Pete slammed the door shut and dropped a wooden bar in place. He walked over and put the dishpan on the table.

"Yo' sho' 'nuff welcome," he said. "Set in that chair over there. Y' hongry?"

"I ate just before the ruckus started."

"Wiltse's sayin' you shot Hilton."

"I know. But Wiltse shot him. Is he dead?"

Pete Randle shook his kinky head. "He ain't dead, but the doc ain't holdin' out much hope for him. He bled a heap. Shot through the lung. He ain't said a solitary word since he got shot and if he dies, looks like Wiltse's lie'll stick."

"Sounds bad," Tracker admitted.

"How'd you get out, suh, if I may ask?"

"Hilton was going to let me go, right after you and Jess left. He had just opened the door when Wiltse stepped in. Ira went for his gun and Wiltse shot him. I dove through the window." Tracker turned his foot sideways. "He shot the heel off my boot."

"Man, that was close!" Pete exclaimed. "What you gonna do now, Mist' Tracker?"

"I've got a gun," Tracker said. "I jumped a man on the roof of the building next to the hotel and took his gun. But I'd like my own pistol. It's in Ira's desk. And I'd like that little bay gelding of mine in the livery stable."

"You stay right here," Pete Randle drawled. "I'll get 'em fo' you, suh."

"And a canteen of water, Pete. I'm riding out of town."

Pete smiled. "An' I betcha you comin' back, suh, right?"

"Right."

Tracker barred the door after Pete Randle slipped out into the night. He waited fifteen minutes, tense, agonizing minutes while the yells increased.

When he had decided that Pete had run into trouble there was a tap on the door. Tracker asked the knocker to sound off and to his relief found it was Randle. He opened the door and stepped out into the darkness, pulling the door shut.

"I had to make a fuss," Randle said. "I pulled 'em off the livery stable but they'll be along any minute. You gettin' out jus' in time."

Tracker stepped up into the saddle. He looked down at the lank Negro. "Thanks, Pete," he said. "I won't forget it."

"You jus' take care," Pete said, grinning up at him.

Tracker put the bay straight away from town, through the sand and cactus, his way lighted by a dim quarter moon. He had one burning question that had to be answered: What had happened to Frank and Pat Cady?

He meant to find out.

CHAPTER 11

The Apache known as *Tatsa* pulled up his pony at a dead campfire. There were the remains of a horse and two Apaches near the fire. Three other dead Indians were in the immediate vicinity. The buzzards that had led him here circled endlessly in the blue sky above him.

He slipped easily to the ground and stared around with rage. This man Tracker would pay dearly for this, he vowed. He squatted and swept the black hair from his head, revealing a gleaming bald head above the curved hook of a nose, and shook sand from the wig. He returned it to his head and worked it into place and stood upright, looking up into the blue sky at the lazily floating black birds.

He felt the freedom that only this wild life could bring. The civilization of Arnold True did not exist out here. Here he was *Tatsa*, leader of the *tendi*, the people. He used them as he used all his resources. The *tendi* were precious to him, for they were a tool of terror that gave him unlimited power. He bent them to his will with promises of a return to greatness which he did not believe himself. But he needed them, and now Tracker had given death to five of his smartest, bravest warriors. The big man would pay dearly, he promised himself again. He vaulted lightly to the bare back of his pony and turned him toward the house on the desert where he lived as a white man, with white men, commanding them with a honed cruelty that gave him no rest.

He found peace only with a loin cloth on his hips and the thigh-length leggings of his ancestors on his feet. He felt the agony of spirit that was his when he thought of the black hair he had to buy. He kept the blond hair of his head shaved, never allowing it to become a discernible growth.

It was late afternoon when he raised the adobe hacienda north of Mule Creek. He turned his pony into the corral and walked through the secret entrance of the walled hacienda, into the secret room, where none had ever been, save himself. He changed into the dark business garb he affected, and then went on into the big, main room, where his men were gathered, drinking, playing cards, telling jokes, and awaiting his arrival.

They fell silent at his entrance, an uneasy silence.

True always had difficulty adjusting when he returned from the desert. It was as though with the change of garb, something of the Apache remained, something that showed, something that was revealed to any who would look.

His black eyes picked out Leo James and commanded him to speak.

"He's in jail in Mule Creek," Leo said triumphantly.

"Where's Shag?"

Leo shifted uncomfortably and looked around the room but got no help from the four men. He let his gaze go back to True. "I dunno, Arnie. He wants to kill Tracker the worst way."

Looking at all of them with contempt, True said, "I want two men here. One outside the window and one outside the door. If she gets away I'll kill you both myself." He leveled a finger at one man and then another. "You two are elected. The rest of us are going into town and take Tracker out of jail."

"What'll Ira Hilton say about that?" Leo asked anxiously.

"I'm not worried about Hilton."

"What about Kirby Landers?" Leo asked, and smilingly added, "I mean Jason Andrews."

A thin, cruel smile touched True's lips. "We've got his horses, haven't we?"

"Well, they're in the north holdin' corral," Leo admitted. "But he thinks we're gonna take him in."

"He'll not be taken in," True said.

"In that case him and that lil yaller-headed filly will be leavin'," Leo said.

True looked thoughtfully at Leo James. "We can use the woman," he said. "We'll let Shag have her for a week. Then she'll work out for us."

"Shag ain't interested in no woman until Tracker is brought down."

"Then after Tracker is dead, Shag can have her," True said. "Let's take care of our business." He strode toward the door and the others followed.

Tracker's sense of direction unerringly led him in a great circle until he was on the road which he'd entered Mule Creek on. It seemed a long time ago. He put the bay into a mile-eating lope, heading east. He sagged in the saddle, exhausted with the night's furious exertions, and the bay cantered on, his body rhythmically pounding out the miles.

Under a ghostly saguaro, he swung down, his practised fingers going over the bay. Not too hot for the amount of work he'd done tonight. Tracker wet his neckerchief and used it to sponge off the bay's nostrils and let him nuzzle a few drops of water in his hand. He sipped sparingly from the canteen and then leather complained as he stepped in the saddle again and went on. He followed the road in the dim light and a gray dawn was pinching the eastern sky when he reined off the road where Cady and his daughter Pat had camped.

The wind was rising again. The sky brightened. The land around was revealed to him, a series of sand-covered ridges, spotted with mesquite, cactus and bear grass. The gray ash of the campfire and scattered camp gear pulled at him.

The camp was just about as he had left it. The coffee pot was overturned and the contents had dried out in the greedy, sucking soil, the grounds stiff to his touch.

He ground-anchored the bay and left him to walk a wide circle around the camp. It was the flutter of buzzards that gave him a clue—that and the odor. The awkward, ugly birds took to the air as he threw sticks at them.

His stomach revolted when he looked at what was left of Frank Cady. He turned his back on the pitiable sight and searched for Pat, though he felt certain she wasn't around. He called a few times and his voice was lost on the lonely desert.

He went back to Cady and spent more than two hours lugging stones for a cairn. When he finally left, he knew the buzzards wouldn't be able to get at the body.

He watered the bay in the spring and mounted and started him down the road, toward Felipe and Maria Ortiz's adobe at the forks of the road. He got there shortly after noon.

Maria was hanging wash from a line in back of the adobe. He ground-anchored the bay and walked around to the back and she greeted him shyly. He helped her hang the wash and it fluttered blue and white in the wind as they walked into the house.

"Felipe is sleeping," she said. "He came home late last night. He says there is much trouble for you in Mule Creek." She glanced at him, adding, "I am very sorry."

Inside the house, the plump baby with huge brown eyes and fat cheeks peered at him from under the table. She screwed her face up like a wrinkled prune and began crying. Maria hurried to the baby and plucked her from the floor and sat her on her ample hip. She moved from fireplace to table to cupboard and soon there were the inevitable tortillas and beans waiting for him.

He sat at the table and began to eat. He was surprised to find that he was hungry, for he hadn't eaten since the night before. He was nearly through when Felipe came from the bedroom, yawning and stretching. He stopped in the middle of a yawn, staring at Tracker.

"This is the gentleman," Maria explained, "who stopped before. The one I spoke of."

Felipe grinned, nodding. He was a small, wiry man with very black hair growing to his shoulders. He wore a white shirt, peon's trousers, and sandals on his dusky feet. He shook hands with Tracker and sat at the table, watching him curiously.

"The soldiers," he said, "they also look for you, sir."

Tracker nodded, though he was puzzled by the information. He couldn't understand Arnie True having that much influence with the Army. Of course, if O'Donnel, the commanding officer of the remount station, was involved in True's unlawful activities, that would account for his interest in trying to bring Tracker down. The big man shook his head perplexedly. "I can't figure out why," he said.

Felipe grinned. "I listen with my ears, sir," he said. "People talk around me as though I were a stump. This man True has told Major O'Donnel that you are an Army investigator, and that you must be stopped at all costs."

That could well be, Tracker thought. Arnie True didn't miss any bets. He was a crafty, cunning man who ran a well-oiled machine that had only one flaw—Leo James. James was trying, Tracker felt sure, to eliminate True and assume the mantle of king of the mountain. Tracker brought his thoughts back to the nearest problem, Pat Cady.

"The other night Leo James and I spooked a horse herd at the springs down the road," Tracker explained. "When I left, the owner of the horses, Frank Cady, told me he would hold them there for a few days." As Tracker talked the smile left Felipe's face. "I saw some of those horses in Mule Creek yesterday," Tracker went on. "I came by the springs this morning. Cady had been shot. His daughter is missing."

"There is much that is bad in this country, sir," Felipe muttered.

"You tell him, Felipe," Maria commanded. "Tell him, my husband."

Felipe shook his head. "There is not much to tell," he said slowly. "I know little, guess much.

The men come in the night. There is much shooting. Two of the men drive the horses to Mule Creek. One man takes the girl to a cabin on Dos Diablos Creek."

"You saw this yourself?"

"No, sir. I got there before the wind covered the sign. I read the sign well, sir. I did not know of Mr. Cady's death until you told me."

"Where is Dos Diablos?"

"In the mountains. This cabin belong to Mr. True. His men bringing horses from Kingman usually hold them there overnight."

Maria placed food before him and he began to eat, talking as he ate, waving his hands, describing the route to the cabin. "After getting into Pesos Canyon, there can be no going wrong," he concluded. "And Pesos is the biggest one of three canyons, the only one that has a stream. It is sometimes dry at this time of the year."

Tracker rose. "Then I guess I'll be going, Felipe."

"Where to, sir?"

"To Dos Diablos," Tracker said grimly. "Where else?"

CHAPTER 12

Tracker rode north. The land began to change, always rising, broken by ridges and gullies that rose higher into round-topped mountains. The sun dipped swiftly toward the horizon, and the shadow of horse and man lay long on the land broken by mesquite, cactus and occasionally a stunted pine.

He stopped at dusk to let the bay rest. He rubbed down the sweaty legs and let the animal nuzzle water from his hand. He stoppered the canteen, wiped the sweat from his face and neck and squatted beside the horse building a smoke with swift, sure fingers. He smoked the cigaret down to his fingers and leather creaked as he mounted and turned upward.

The moon rose early and the wind died away. The only sound was the creak of the saddle and the soft muffled thud of the bay's hooves.

It was well after dark when he reached the summit and the three canyons spread out, rising tunnel dark, in the silvery light. He didn't halt, but put the bay across the dry, sandy wash and into Pesos, the largest of the three canyons. There was a fairly well-defined trail up the canyon.

The canyon widened, though there was little growth. The creek bed was dry except for an occasional scummy pool. The canyon turned and the grade steepened. The bay labored upward. The air began to cool and he caught a brief scent of pine on a sudden gust of wind. The horse quickened his step as though he sensed the end of a journey.

He emerged from the canyon and found that the trail skirted the edge of the round-topped mountain he'd seen earlier from below. There was some ponderosa pine here and he breathed the fragrance deeply, as memories returned of his somewhat similar home country. He let the bay walk, choose his own pace, while he scanned the trail ahead.

He didn't want to blunder into True's cabin. He passed between a huge rock beside the trail directly across from which was a towering pine. He heard a shell jacked into a chamber and he stopped the bay.

"Just hold it right there." Leo James stepped from behind the tree, a wide grin on his face. He looked up at the top of the rock. "All right, Cordie, come on down."

A man slid down the rock and landed catlike on his feet, holding the rifle on Tracker. "Get down off that horse," he said. Cordie was a hump-shouldered cowboy and in the moonlight his eyes looked mean and ornery.

Tracker felt like reining around and running for it, but there wasn't a chance. The moonlight was too bright and the trail ran in open country, along the side of the mountain. Cordie looked like a man who'd enjoy pot shooting at him as he ran. He stepped to the ground.

"Get out ahead," Cordie said, motioning with the rifle.

"Get that gun o' his, Cordie," Leo James ordered, "before he gets any funny notions."

"I wish he would," Cordie grunted, but he leaned over and yanked the Colt from Tracker's holster.

Tracker walked on ahead, his heart beating faster. Neither of them had noticed the extra gun jammed in his belt. It was the gun he'd taken from the man on the roof, back at Mule Creek. As he walked, he opened his shirt, slipped the gun inside and buttoned the shirt.

They were at the cabin. Sam Tracker had a glimpse of a rough pole fence, in the rear of the cabin, closing off a shallow box canyon. There were four horses behind the poles. *Two more around somewhere,* Tracker thought; *or two extra horses.*

"Go on in. Open the door and go in," James ordered.

Tracker pushed the door open and looked in. There was a single candle burning on the small table in the center of the room. The table held a whiskey bottle and a deck of cards. A double decker bunk was built in one corner, a rusty stove stood in another, and an apple box nailed to the wall served as a cupboard. Tracker looked at the bunk again. Pat lay on the bottom bunk, with strands of a lariat circling her arms, holding her arms tight against her body. Her hair was a tangle under her head. Her eyes were open and widened as he came into the room, into the illumination of the candle. Then she saw the man behind Tracker holding the rifle on him, and she closed her eyes, her face wrinkling.

"You all right, Pat?" Tracker asked.

"Why, sure, she's all right," Leo James said, circling Tracker and seating himself at the table. He uncorked the whiskey bottle and took a drink. "She's jes' fine. We been takin' real good care o' her, ain't we, Cordie?"

"Do you have to tie her up?" Tracker asked, giving James a contemptuous glance. "Or maybe you're afraid she might take your pelt?"

"Oh, we jes' tied her up when one o' the boys heard you comin'," Leo said. "Let her loose, Cordie."

Cordie stood the rifle beside the bed and leaned over and lifted Pat out and stood her on her feet. He unwound the lariat and coiled it up and tossed it in a corner. He picked up his rifle and crossed the room and opened the door and disappeared.

Pat rubbed her arms, glancing over at Tracker who stood quietly. Leo James was watching them alertly, sitting at the table riffling the cards.

Tracker moved over to the table, took one of the

148

chairs and carried it to the bunk and Pat Cady sat in it. He leaned against the bunk looking down at her. "I'm sorry about your pop," he said.

She kept her voice low. "Papa didn't have a chance."

Tracker jerked his head toward James. "Was he in on it?"

Leo James heard. "No, I wasn't, Tracker."

She shook her head. "There were three men, two besides Cordie. The other two drove off the horses after the shooting. Cordie brought me here. That fat man got here later, with two other men whose names I don't know." She put her head in her hands and though she didn't make a sound, Tracker knew she was crying. He felt a savage fury well up inside him.

He felt something else, too. Something physical; the pistol pressing against his belly. Leo James sat at the table looking at him warily but with assurance that help was near. Three other men were nearby, within calling distance. Tracker had a feeling of frustration, not knowing exactly what went on. He was reluctant to make a break against unpredictable odds. Besides, he wanted to find out as much as possible about the puzzling events in and around Mule Creek. If Leo James had him, Tracker, marked for a bullet, the fat man might be inclined to reveal some of the shadowy happenings.

He drifted over to the table and sat down across

from James. He reached for the bottle. "Mind if I have a snort?"

"Don't mind if you do," Leo James said. "It might be your last. Then again I don't know." He riffled the cards idly. "Damn disappointed in you, Tracker. I had it all set up for you to make some money and get well and you go hi-falutin' all over hell'n gone."

Tracker tilted the bottle. He didn't drink much but he kept the bottle to his lips for an appreciable time. He lowered the bottle to the table and wiped his lips with the back of his left hand. "Your plans kind of went haywire, Leo."

The fat man slipped down in his chair, his slitted eyes on Tracker's face. "Plans go haywire," he said. "That's why I always got a couple for everything, Tracker."

"You'll come off second best in a fight with Arnie True," Tracker observed and detected a touch of resentment in James's eyes. "He's one man you can't beat, because he's smarter than you. Do you think for a moment he doesn't know what you're up to?"

"Go on talkin', horse wrangler," James said. "You're so damn smart."

"I know what you tried to do," Tracker went on. "You figured to get Arnie out of the way and have me take the blame for it. What I'd like to know is why."

"Arnie thought he had you in his hand," James

said idly. "He was set to take you out of jail and cut you up in little pieces. When he got there and you had broke jail I thought he'd have a fit. What'd you do to make him put a price on you?"

"I wouldn't know," Tracker said. "I'm a horse rancher. You know all about that because I told you. How much does Arnie True offer?"

"He offered five hundred for you dead," Leo said with relish, "but a cool thousand for you alive. I guess he wants to take care o' you, personal like."

"You said he's part Apache," Tracker said.

"That's right. He ain't foolin' me none. I know he dresses up in that Indian outfit and goes out and meets his own."

"A bald-headed Apache," Tracker scoffed.

"Yeah, well, he even takes care o' that. He'd kill me if he thought I knew, but he's got a head o' black hair he puts on, just like you put on a hat."

Tracker laughed. "James, you been smoking some of that weed they get from Mexico, or eating peyote."

James uncorked the bottle and took another long pull. He put the bottle down without offering it to Tracker. "Me and Arnie never did get along. He treats me like a dog."

"Maybe you are a dog. Do you think you can wean all Arnie's men away from him?"

James laughed but there was a tinge of anger in his laughter. "Wean 'em away? All Arnie had left was Wiltse and Crewe. And Wiltse's out o' his head, can't think of nothin' but shootin' you right through your belly button."

He looked angry. "Arnie didn't never treat the major right, either. Didn't give him his fair cut and he's ready to part ways with Arnie. Fact is, Arnie ain't got nobody on his side and I'll finish him up when the time comes."

"You'll all be finished, Leo," Tracker said, "just as soon as Territorial officials get my letter."

Leo James clutched his stomach with both hands, chortling with soft laughter. "Your letter! That's the funniest damn thing I ever heard. Ain't nobody gonna get no letter from you, Tracker."

Tracker felt a sudden chill around his heart but he didn't betray his emotions.

Leo James gave him a wicked glance. "Know why, horse wrangler? Because Arnie caught that gal writing your letter. He's got her under lock and key! Ain't nobody gonna hear from you, Tracker, unless you call the buzzards somebody!"

For just a fraction of a second Tracker thought of Jean Rainey being locked in some room, alone and friendless. His hand snaked inside his shirt and came out with the Colt.

Leo James's mouth fell open. He put out his hand imploringly, frightened at the look on Tracker's face. "Don't shoot me, Tracker," he begged, "don't shoot me!"

For a second Tracker's hand tightened on the

trigger and then relaxed. "Don't give me a reason, Leo." He walked around James and lifted his gun. He nodded to Pat and she glided to his side. He gave her James's gun. "Stand by the door. Listen sharp and let me know if anybody comes."

She took the gun and went to the door.

"On your feet, Leo," Tracker said, jabbing him with the gun. "Get on the bunk, fat man. You'll get the same treatment you gave Pat." He shoved James toward the bunk, rapped him behind the ear with the Colt and then guided his body into the bed.

He used the same rope that Cordie had taken from Pat and tied James up securely. He took off James's neckerchief and knotted it in the middle and forced the knot into the fat man's mouth and tied it behind his head. Then he snuffed out the candle and walked to the door and stood beside Pat.

"Where's the other three?"

"There's three trails into here," she said. "One on each trail."

"How far away, or do you know?"

"I don't know. It can't be far, though."

"Stay close to me and keep quiet."

He opened the cabin door but didn't go out at once. The land out there before him was dotted with trees and rocks, and fell steeply away to the maze of shallow canyons below. Moonlight shadowed the area and nothing moved in his range of sight.

He stepped outside, keeping close to the cabin wall and waited until she was close to him. He began edging toward the corner and on reaching it, peered around. His own horse stood near the pole enclosure. The area between him and his horse was open and light. He pulled her close and whispered, "Maybe you better stay here while I bring the horses up."

She didn't answer but squeezed his arm.

He considered the open space again and then went out at a loping run, his pistol ready, his nerves taut, his finger on the trigger. The horse raised his head and nervously side-stepped as Tracker neared him. Tracker soothed him with a few words and stood close in the shadow of the horse and looked over the pole enclosure. One horse stood near, evidently seeking the companionship of the bay, while the others were back in the shadows. He could hear them cropping grass.

His bay was still saddled. Four saddles topped the pole fence a dozen feet from him. Two of them were cavalry saddles. He shook his head in puzzled irritation, not knowing what to make of this. Maybe two of the soldiers assigned to the remount station were here to help deliver horses to the Army. But that couldn't be; Major O'Donnel's thievery must be administrative. He wouldn't be so foolish as to bring his enlisted men into his deals. Enlisted men were prone to drink and talk too much. Besides, they were moved around from one post to another so much, a commanding officer couldn't be certain how long he'd retain any certain man. O'Donnel hadn't impressed him as a fool—an overly cautious man, but certainly not foolish. It must so happen, Tracker thought, that two of Leo's men had cavalry saddles and that was it.

Yet, it was strange; and Tracker distrusted strange facts. He put these details out of his mind though, under pressures of the moment. At any time one of the three might come in on him. He stepped to the riding gear and selected a bridle at random. He crawled through the enclosure and approached the horse standing with raised head and erect ears. The horse permitted him to get close enough for the strange odor and then wheeled. But Tracker, anticipating the movement, leaped and got a hand on the fetlock and pulled the head down and slipped the bit into the clenched teeth and then forced them open. He finished bridling the horse, a rangy roan gelding and led him to the saddles, selected a blanket and smoothed it on. He threw on the first saddle he reached for, one of the McClellans. He cinched it down and led the horse along the pole fence, looking for a gate.

He found it, a simple set of bars. He slipped the

pole bars out of the slot and let them drop on the ground. He led the roan through and back to his own horse. He untied the reins of the bay and led the two horses to the cabin and helped Pat mount the tall gelding. He gave the bay's reins to her and led her horse into the opposite and shadowed end of the cabin.

"Stay out of sight here," he ordered. "I'll whistle like this." He put his fingers in his mouth and gave a fair imitation of a night bird's call. "You hear that, come in a hurry."

He moved slowly out, seeking the moonshade, moving like a shadow. He edged away from the trail, seeking an easy way to the high rock on which Cordie had been posted when he came up the trail. He heard a horse whinny, heard Pat's cry and he whirled and raced for the cabin.

A yellow lance of flame leaped out at him and he threw himself on the ground, rolled over as a bullet spat gravel where he had been a moment before. He triggered a shot at the dark shape, rather than a solid target. He heard the grunt and the shape whirled away and down.

Tracker got to his knees and then his feet, went in edgily, watching for movement, his pistol cocked and ready. He kicked a dropped gun aside and knelt for a moment. His bullet had hit Cordie's throat, ripping his neck open and the blood still pumped out in a gushing stream.

He managed to pick up the reins from Pat and

mounted the excited bay. He said, "I hope he's the one from below," and touched spurs to the bay and they went away in a rush.

He spurred hard, stretching the bay's stride until they were in a pounding gallop. The tall pine and rock loomed up on the trail and then they thundered past and no bullet greeted or chased them. He heard the sound of an owl in the timber above. He pulled the willing bay in to an easy canter. Pat surged up alongside of him.

"I can hear horses," she said, "following us."

"They wouldn't have time to saddle up," he said quietly. "I left the bars down. Their horses are following us."

They rode in silence through the shadowy canyon. The moon was gone but the sky was clear and bright with stars. The mountains around them were dark and mysterious and seemed to be waiting, listening. The hours caught up with Tracker and he sagged in the saddle. The girl rode beside him and slightly to the rear, watching the weary slump of his body.

After a time she spoke. "Maybe we better stop and rest."

He came erect at the sound of her voice. "No, we'll go on for a while. I suspect there were horses due at the cabin. That means more men, too. Let's put some miles behind us."

"You like that girl?" she asked.

"What girl?"

"The one who wrote the letter—and got caught doing it."

"Yeah, I like her all right, I suppose."

"Like? All right? You should have seen your face when Leo James told you that fellow had her." There was a tinge of jealousy in her voice.

"What about my face? It's ugly enough as it is."

"Ugly? You're the handsomest man I ever met."

"You're kind of young," he observed.

"Young in years, yes. But I know. And when Leo James said what he did I thought you'd tear him apart. I thought to myself then that you are sweet on her."

Tracker laughed.

"That's the nastiest laugh I've ever heard," she declared.

"A nasty thought brought it on," he answered.

The canyon gradually flattened and they came out of the sandy draw and Tracker headed directly south. In the distance he could see a clump of trees that marked water and he headed the tired horses in that direction. The horses, smelling water, quickened their pace.

Tracker held up his hand and they stopped. Saddle leather creaked as he stepped to the ground and handed his reins to Pat. "Stay here while I scout that spring. I don't want us to walk in on anybody I know."

Tracker went a dozen feet from the horses. He waited, listening. After a while he went ahead, moving slowly, making no noise at all as he approached the grove. Even in the darkness he could see through the sparse growth that surrounded the spring. It appeared to be empty, but he went through it from north to south and then whistled the soft notes of the night bird and heard the horses move in.

He unsaddled and let the horses drink. He rubbed them down, using wisps of grass growing tall around the spring. Pat started to gather firewood but he stopped her.

"We've nothing to cook, anyway," he said. "And we don't want to advertise we're here." He put the horses on picket and got the blanket roll from his saddle. "I've just one blanket, you take it."

"Why can't we both use it?" she asked.

He spread the blanket out for her, placing part of it over the saddle for a pillow. "I guess you're younger than I thought," he said gruffly. "Just how old are you, Pat?"

"S—seventeen."

He looked at her, amused. "Why didn't you say eighteen?"

"Why, that's old!" she exclaimed. "A girl is practically an old maid at eighteen!"

He carried his saddle a distance from the blanket and lay down, feeling the ache of his muscles, the tiredness of his body. He put his hat beside him and looked up through the trees at the sky which was beginning to lighten. He gave himself up to the renewal that sleep and rest brought, falling asleep instantly.

He awakened once, when he felt something warm snuggled up to him and the blanket covered them both.

CHAPTER 13

Before morning he was up. He left Pat sleeping and walked away from the spring, down to where it trickled off into nothingness, absorbed by the sand. He saw a rabbit sitting on its hind legs nibbling at something it held between its forepaws. He drew his gun and aimed it at the rabbit and then slowly replaced it in the holster.

Looking about, he found a thick chunk of wood. Slowly, he reached for it, picked it up and hurled it, knocking the rabbit down. He ran over there and grasped its hind legs and used the flat of his hand to dispose of it, directing a sharp crack behind the ears.

He started a fire and while it burned to the right proportion for roasting, he cleaned and skinned out the rabbit. He spitted it and placed the ends of the stick over two forked sticks on each side of the fire. By the time he had it ready, the fire was a hot bed of coals. He made a cigaret and smoked it while he turned the stick that held the rabbit so it would cook evenly. He cleaned his pocket knife and walked to the spring and splashed cold water on his face. He used his neckerchief to dry with. The horses whinnied at him. Birds sang in the trees. He turned to find Pat sitting up in the tangle of blanket, yawning, watching him through the yawn.

"Sleep good?"

She nodded. "I—I hope I didn't disturb you. I couldn't help it. I felt so lonely and all. Maybe scared, too. Do you think I'm a sissy?"

"For being scared?" He shook his head. "No. I've been scared a time or two."

"You!" She stared at him with wide blue eyes. "You're making fun of me."

"Not so's you could notice," he smiled. "Anybody who isn't crazy gets scared."

"Have you really?"

"Fear has kept many a man alive," he said. "It feeds juice to your heart and steps up your alertness. It makes a person stronger, to fight or run as common sense dictates. So fear isn't such a bad thing after all. Unless it paralyzes you." He nodded to the creek. "Go wash up. Breakfast is nearly ready."

She wrinkled her nose, sniffing. "Smells good, too." She rose and walked to the creek and knelt and washed her face and hands. She pulled the tail of her shirt out and dried her hands with it and patted her face dry. She saw him watching her and self-consciously tucked the shirt back into her jeans. She came back to the fire and knelt there and accepted the juicy piece of roasted rabbit he gave her.

"Where are we going?"

He'd thought about that. It was closer to Hamilton's Rafter H than the Ortiz place at the forks. He'd decided during the ride that it would be Hamilton's. He'd lay it on the line to Jess, for help, manpower—guns if need be—to free Jean Rainey from Arnie True, and for recovering his herd. Provided, Kirby Landers hadn't disposed of them in the meantime. "A friend's ranch," he said. "Jess Hamilton. I can leave you there while I take care of some important business."

"Like getting that girl loose?"

He nodded. "And getting my horse herd back."

She stared at him. "Your horse herd?"

He told her the story as they ate the roasted rabbit, which even without salt tasted good. "My partner stole my share of all the horses and money we had. He even took the girl I was going to marry." He smiled wryly. "I trailed him to Mule Creek. I was on his trail, close, when I spooked your horses.

"The earth seemed to swallow him up at Mule Creek. It so happened that an old friend has a ranch near there. That's where we're going. I went on out to see Jess Hamilton and tried to borrow some money from him. I needed it to fill my contract with the Army at Coyotero. Jess didn't have it to loan, so he said. But I ran into Christine Benton out there. She was the girl I was going to marry. Jess had found her on the trail when Kirby Landers abandoned her."

"She slowed him down?"

Tracker nodded. "I took her into town with me,

after Jess and I had a fight with Crewe and Wiltse. Crewe got killed. Afterward, in town, Christine saw Kirby and told me. I had a fight with him and just when I had him where he was ready to talk, the sheriff walked in. The sheriff arrested me and put me in jail. I had talked him into letting me go when Wiltse, one of True's gunmen, walked in, wanting to kill me. He shot the sheriff but I managed to get away. Now everybody thinks I killed the sheriff. The law is looking for me—Wiltse got appointed to act as sheriff—and Arnie True and his outlaws are after me, too."

"But what about Jean Rainey?" Pat asked. "Where'd you meet up with her?"

"She works for Arnie True," Tracker said uncomfortably. "I met her a couple of times. She's a singer. True tricked her into coming to Mule Creek to work in the Bird Cage Saloon. As soon as she found out what singing in a saloon meant, she quit. True gave her a job as bookkeeper. I met her in his office. Then she came to see me in jail. That's when she agreed to write the letters for me. True found out and is holding her until this is over."

She was looking at him strangely, with two bright red spots in her cheeks, her blue eyes flashing. "Maybe she wanted to be discovered," she said. "Maybe she's using that as a means of getting the money to get back where she come from."

"I don't think so."

"Men," she said in disgust. She finished her breakfast in silence and as Tracker saddled, she spoke her thoughts. "I'd never double-cross a man I loved."

"I'm sure you wouldn't." He glanced at her and stopped abruptly the act of cinching down a saddle. Her blue eyes were filled with tears. "What's wrong?"

She hurriedly wiped her eyes with her finger tips. "Darn it," she muttered. "I just wish somebody would turn into a ring-tailed wampus cat for me."

He didn't laugh. He put his arm around her shoulders and pulled her against him. "Someone will," he said. "Someone will, Pat. You can bet on that." He released her and finished saddling and they mounted and rode out of the grove.

They rode all through the hot, shimmering day, resting the horses twice. Evening was near as Tracker and Pat approached the Rafter H. It had been a silent ride, each busy with his own thoughts. Now as the shadows grew longer, the world became even quieter. The slightest sound traveled easily in the clear air of the desert country. This was a land of sky and sand and it was unfamiliar to Tracker. He didn't like it. He liked best the lift of the high country, the cool air, the fragrance of pine and cedar. He even thought the sky was a darker blue to the north, where his ranch lay waiting for his return. *If I return,* he thought with some bitterness.

The iron triangle at the cookshack was banging lustily as they rode into the yard. It was dark enough for a light to show through the window. They dismounted and Tracker tied the horses and together they walked around to the kitchen door in the back. The door was standing open and Tracker rapped on the door frame.

Jess Hamilton appeared in the doorway. He had an apron around his middle and the smell of cooking food wafted out the door and caused the saliva to flow in Tracker's mouth.

"Sam! Well, come on in . . ." He saw Pat then and his hand went automatically to his head which was bare.

"This is Pat Cady, Jess," Tracker said, standing aside for Pat to enter. She went into the kitchen with Jess staring at her.

Briefly, he told Jess what had happened since he'd last seen him.

"Well, I'll be dad-burned," Jess blurted when he was through.

Pat took the apron from around Jess and donned it herself. "You two go talk," she said. "I'll finish getting supper."

Jess and Tracker sat at the kitchen table, smoking and talking. Pat worked efficiently but quietly and she listened eagerly to what they had to say.

Jess was evasive and uneasy at first. Then he told Tracker what was bothering him. "There's been two posses out lookin' for you," he said. "Right here, Sam. Second one searched the ranch. I don't like bein' held at gunpoint and my ranch shook down."

Tracker ignored the reproach in Jess's voice. "How's Ira Hilton?"

Jess shook his head. "Not too well. Doc don't expect him to hang on much longer."

"You don't think I tried to kill him, do you, Jess?"

"I don't know what to think, Sam," Jess answered. "All I know is I don't want to get crossways with Arnie True."

"When a bully runs the country," Tracker said coolly, "you do one of two things: take anything the bully hands out, or fight him."

Jess put his hands out helplessly.

"You haven't made a decision yet, Jess," Tracker said softly. "Why not? You wouldn't have hesitated back in the days when you were riding for Crook."

"Things change," Jess said wearily. "Men, too. It's different now, Sam. I had my life to lose then and nothing else. Now . . ." He looked around. ". . . now, I think every step of the way. When I worked for the Army they fed and clothed me and gave me a hundred dollars a month. I could blow it in, in one night on the town, and I knew I'd eat for the next month. Now I got six men working for me. I hafta dig up their wages every month whether I'm makin' it or not. Seems like all I'm doin' is working for those six cowboys."

"I can see I'm not going to get any help from you," Tracker said.

"What can I do?" Jess asked angrily.

"You got a crew."

"I got a crew to run a ranch, not fight with True's gunslingers."

"They'll do what they're told," Tracker said. "Fact is, they wouldn't need much urging."

"I'm not tellin' them to go against True's guns," Jess said grimly. "I got too much to lose."

"You might find yourself in the middle of it," Tracker pointed out, "whether you like it or not."

"What do you mean by that?"

"Right now, Wiltse thinks I killed Crewe. If it got out that you pulled the trigger, Wiltse would be as hot for you as he is for me."

"I know you better than that," Jess Hamilton said.

"A man up against something that won't give is apt to change," Tracker retorted. "However, you're right. I wouldn't do it and I'm not going to ask you again, Jess, except for one thing."

"What's that?"

"Don't sound so damn suspicious. I want you to keep Pat here until the smoke dies down."

"That's fine with me," Hamilton said and as Pat placed food on the table they pushed their chairs up. "Um, um, looks mighty fine."

Pat seated herself with them. She looked at Tracker with flushed cheeks and her eyes were bright. "I won't stay," she announced. "You wanted him to help and he wouldn't. If he won't help you, I won't stay here." She turned her smoky gaze from Tracker to Hamilton. "And you can put that in your pipe and smoke it!"

Jess gulped. "I—uh, well, you see, miss . . ."

"Never mind the reasons," she said. "If your places were changed, if you were in trouble, what do you suppose Sam would say when you asked for help? Did you think of that?" She threw down her fork and pushed back her chair and ran out the door.

Jess looked at Tracker helplessly. "Well, she's got a mind of her own," he said.

"She's pretty wrought up, Jess," Tracker said mildly. "But there's something in what she says."

Jess slapped the table with his open palm. "Damn it, don't I know that?" he asked. "I'm ashamed of myself, Sam, believe me. But damn, what can I do?"

"That's a question," Tracker answered, "you'll have to answer all by your lonesome."

The door was open and Pat Cady came flying through like a projectile. She halted inside the door, her breath coming in gasps, her chest heaving. She looked at Tracker. "Riders coming fast!" she said.

CHAPTER 14

Tracker grabbed her hand as he went out the door, pulling her after him. He slipped around the house to the north as the riders swept up to the kitchen door from the south.

"Fan out." Shag Wiltse's voice was curt. The creak of leather spoke of movement from the saddle. "Shoot anybody that leaves the house."

Horsemen moved out away from the house and encircled it. Pressed against the wall, Tracker and Pat watched one man ride out a distance, turn, stop and sit watchfully in the saddle.

The voice of Shag Wiltse came clearly through the unplaned boards of the square two-story house. "Got company, Hamilton?"

"Had a couple of the boys up for supper," Jess Hamilton said.

"Why don't you eat with your riders?" Wiltse asked.

Jess Hamilton laughed, a forced laugh that made Tracker grind his teeth. What in the world had happened to Jess, the Hamilton he knew in the old days? "Reckon Curly York's about the worst cook in the country," he said. "But don't let on I said that. His feelin's hurt real easy."

"You can quit lyin', Hamilton." Wiltse's voice deepened. "I'm gonna burn you out if Tracker don't walk out peaceable. By the time I count five." He paused and started counting: "One . . ."

"Stay here," Tracker commanded. Without waiting for Pat's answer, he slipped along the wall to the front and stepped up on the porch, still in the shadows. He stopped to pass under the window and went through the front door standing up. He walked quietly across the room and down the hallway and stepped into the kitchen. He had his Colt in his hand, with the hammer drawn back.

"Keep right on counting, Wiltse," Tracker said. "When you get to five start burning and I'll start shooting."

Wiltse whirled but the gun in Tracker's hand stopped him short, his fingers poised above his gun.

For a long electric moment, everyone froze, and there was death in the air. Then with a sigh, Wiltse relaxed, straightened, and turned toward the door.

"Wait," Tracker said.

His brittle voice stopped Wiltse. He turned his head without turning his body. "You want to stop me," he said, "shoot me in the back." He stepped toward the door again and Tracker eased the hammer down on his pistol and swung the frame against Wiltse's head, a blow that staggered him but didn't knock him down. He pulled Wiltse's gun and shoved the dazed gunfighter into the wall. "Don't go anywhere just yet."

Jess Hamilton regained his voice. "My gawd,

Sam, we're in for it." There was agony of doubt and indecision in his voice. Everything had been going fine for him here until Sam Tracker showed up. Back in the old days he liked Tracker and he still liked him. But now there was a difference; he was wealthy and Tracker had nothing. Tracker had brought him a mess of trouble and there seemed to be no end to it.

Tracker glanced at him with grim foreboding eyes. He was in a dangerous position. He had Wiltse here under his gun, but the others would grow impatient. When Wiltse's men checked there'd be powder burned. "Jess, you're a fool to lie down and let people walk on you. After a while they don't even walk easy."

"I don't want no trouble."

"You've got it, man. That's what's wrong with most people. By trying to avoid trouble they just bring on more."

"No. A man minds his own business and pays his debts . . ."

"Why, Jess, that's exactly what I'm trying to do. Mind my own business. And collecting what's due me, is just as much an obligation as the payoff. I want my horses and my money and hell itself won't stop me."

"You'll collect a bullet," Wiltse said thickly.

There was a scattering of shots outside and the rush of hooves. A rifle blasted in the night and Pat Cady ran into the room. She looked with glowing eyes at Tracker. "They're on the run!" she said gleefully. "They're really cutting out, Sam!"

He stared at her and then his eyes went to the door as Curly York came in, with a rifle held ready. There was an occasional shot outside; the drumming hooves receded into the distance, finally dying out completely.

"Boss, you all right?" Curly asked in a worried voice.

"Hell, yes, I'm all right," Jess Hamilton said. "What's goin' on out there?"

Curly nodded to Pat Cady. "She come in and told us somebody had you boxed up here. Me an' the boys shooed 'em off, that's all."

"Damn, the fat's in the fire now," Hamilton said. He looked morosely at Tracker. "What's the next move, Sam?"

Wiltse raised his head, his eyes glowing a baleful green. "Whatever it is, it's gonna be his last."

Tracker ignored him. "I'm going to Mule Creek," Tracker said. "I expect Wiltse will show me where Miss Rainey is being kept."

"Sure, Tracker," Wiltse said. "I'll show you."

"Don't be a damned fool," Hamilton snapped.

"I want to borrow a horse," Tracker said. "You can keep my bay until I return yours." He moved toward the door. "Keep that rifle on him, Curly."

Wiltse laughed.

"Saddle a horse for me," Pat said as Tracker went through the door. "I'm going with you."

"Most damn foolishness I ever heard of!" Jess said furiously. "If you want to get your head blowed off, go on! But you shouldn't ought to take that girl with you."

"I can take care of myself," Pat flared. "Come on, Sam, I'll help you saddle."

The Rafter H crew was cluttered around the door, looking in. They fell back as Tracker came out, followed by Pat. He caught up the bay and roan and led them down to the corral. He roped two ponies and changed saddles.

Pat mounted and waited until he got into the saddle. They walked their horses back to the house and silently waited while Wiltse climbed stiffly on his horse.

"At least don't go by the road," Hamilton called.

Tracker waved his hand and they moved off into the night.

An hour they rode under the stars, through sandy dunes and through narrow twisting arroyos. Tracker was unfamiliar with the country but he had a wonderfully developed sense of direction. They rode in silence with only the wind, the creak of leather and the soft clump of hooves in the sand breaking the stillness. Tracker paused once and let Pat draw up abreast of him.

"How you making it?" he asked Pat.

"All right, Sam. I can ride all day and then all night. I was born in a saddle, practically."

"Good girl."

Wiltse was silent. The man was gloating at the prospect. This man Tracker was the biggest fool he'd ever come across. He'd take him right to where the Rainey woman was held all right. There'd be a reception committee for him.

The night was warm with the wind from the southwest. The moon was up now and the stars became dimmer. There were few clouds, lenticular in shape in the western sky, far distant, merging with the shadowy outline of the San Jacinto mountains. The horizon was indistinct all around. The wind was rising out there.

"We're turning south and west," Tracker said. "We'll come on Mule Creek from the California side."

They came on the river in the predawn gray. There was an illusion of coolness in the air. They had covered the distance in a roundabout way and Tracker had spared the horses. He halted on the edge of the river, remembering his talk with Jean Rainey, almost at the very spot where they hauled up. It seemed such a long time ago but he remembered her features clearly, the lift of her head, the clearness of her eyes.

"Where's Miss Rainey?"

Wiltse lifted his lip over his yellow teeth. "In

True's house," he said. "Right straight up the river, friend, about two miles."

"From here on you ride close to me."

Tracker looked at Pat. "There's liable to be some trouble. I'd take it as a favor if you'd ride into Mule Creek and find Pete Randle. He's the town barber. Lives in a couple of rooms in back of his shop. Tell him I sent you and want you to stay there until I call for you."

She looked at him steadily. "That the way you want it?" She held up Wiltse's rifle. "I can use this, you know."

"I'll bet you can."

"I can't stand all the waiting," she said. "I don't want you to leave me behind. I can carry my share of the load."

"You don't want to get turned over my knee," he said sternly, "start making tracks for Mule Creek." He watched her frown form and then she smoothed out her face and, with Indianlike impassivity, turned her horse.

Tracker touched spurs to his horse and rode up beside Wiltse. "Let's get on with it," he said.

They rode toward True's ranch. There was a rough trail beside the river and they wound in and out among the willows, the mesquite and a scattering of smoke trees, their dusty foliage moving in the minute breeze from the river.

As they neared the ranch, Tracker stopped. The house was a rambling brown adobe, with a veranda all across the front. The windows were narrow slits in the brown walls. There was an adobe wall enclosing the place and a leafy oak tree showed above the roof.

No smoke came from the chimney.

Four horses looked over the corral fence behind the hacienda. One of the horses whistled a shrill welcome.

"Anybody here?"

"Find out for yourself."

"Whose horses?"

"I don't know."

Tracker motioned Wiltse out ahead of him and followed closely. They stopped at the hitching rail with Wiltse screening Tracker's body. Sam Tracker drew his gun and walked behind Wiltse to the front door. He pressed the muzzle of the gun against Wiltse's back. "Just open the door, go right in, don't make any sudden move."

Wiltse hesitated and then opened the door. It swung in with a sighing creak. The big front room was empty, Tracker saw, as he followed Wiltse closely across the room and out the inner door and along a shaded walk inside a patio. There was a single huge tree in the center of the patio, fed by a spring that bubbled up from close to its roots, into a natural tank which someone had augmented by placing rocks around the bank. The small stream from the spring went across the middle of the patio and disappeared under the adobe wall that joined with the two wings running out from the main house. The entire patio was enclosed except for a single opening close to the other wing. All this Tracker took in as they walked the distance of the wing, where Wiltse stopped before a closed door. He looked at Tracker and nodded to the door.

"Open it and walk in," Tracker said, low-voiced.

Wiltse lifted a door handle and the door swung inward. Tracker, looking over Wiltse's shoulder, saw Jean Rainey sitting in a chair straight across the room from where he stood. Her arms were tied to the arms of the chair, her feet bound and a gag in her mouth. Her eyes seemed enormous, as they darted from side to side.

Pushing ahead of Wiltse, Tracker stepped into the room. He sensed rather than saw the swift motion and dodged. The blow on his head knocked him sprawling to the dirt floor and into black oblivion. He had one lucid thought before he went out and that was Jean Rainey had been trying to signal danger with her eyes.

CHAPTER 15

He awoke but was too sick to care, too sick to help himself. He lay on a pad on the floor and gradually became aware that his head was being bathed and bandaged. He opened one eye when he heard a moan.

Jean Rainey was kneeling beside him, taking care of him.

He gave himself up to the soft ministrations of her hands and then he slept.

It was late afternoon when he awoke. He turned on his belly and pushed himself up, almost crying out aloud with the pain in his head. He felt her arms around him, helping him sit upright, kneeling beside him, her face close, with a smear of dirt on her chin and forehead. Her eyes were steady though concerned.

"How do you feel?"

He touched his bandaged head. "Like I'd been hit with a hammer."

"It was a gun. I tried to warn you. But I was gagged."

"That's about the last thing I knew—that you were trying to warn me. Then the roof fell in." He scrubbed his face with his knuckles. "Kind of stupid of me, riding in wide open like that. But when I heard you were here, only thing I could think of was getting here. When we didn't get any fire, I kept coming."

"I heard Wiltse tell James why you came." She looked at him steadily, and then added, "I'm awfully proud you tried to help me, Sam."

He grinned wryly. "I'm awfully sorry it didn't work out." He moved to a more comfortable position. "I wonder where True is now."

She stared at him. "You don't know? Of course you don't, you couldn't. Arnie True is dead."

He waited in silence, digesting this information, waiting for her to go on.

"Leo James killed him. Or had him killed. I don't think he meant to do it, but Mr. True suspected James of a doublecross and so James had him killed. Leo James is taking over True's empire."

"I figured that," Tracker said. "I was supposed to take the blame for True. But I suppose Hilton getting shot spoiled Leo's plans."

She nodded. "We have another sheriff now, Wiltse."

"Then Hilton died?"

"No, but the doctor still doesn't think Sheriff Hilton will recover. I think James has been urging Wiltse to finish the job." She shivered though it was warm in the room.

Tracker swore softly. "James is wiser—and dirtier—than I thought."

"I can't believe it. James was wild at being tied

up. He cursed and told everyone what he was going to do to you when he finally caught you. He used to appear to me to be a slightly stupid, though good-natured man. He has revealed himself for what he is—a thorough scoundrel, with not an ounce of human kindness in him. He—he's an animal!"

"No more than True. Funny, True took over this country with fear. He took it with a gun. And it was taken away from him the same way." He looked at her. "What's his plans for you? What has Leo James got mapped out for you?"

She frowned at him, her forehead wrinkled. "He has said that he'll break me, Sam. And then use me in the Bird Cage."

He felt a stir of rage and climbed to his feet and walked to the narrow slot in the wall. He could only see a narrow perspective because of the thickness of the wall. He turned and looked at her where she sat on the pad. "A guard on the door?"

She nodded.

"I wonder how many men Leo has?"

"About fifteen, I think. He had his own group of men who were loyal to him, and True had his. Leo James eliminated the ones he couldn't trust and merged the remainder with his own—hands, he called them." She looked away. "Your friend Kirby Landers worked with Leo to take over from True."

"Kirby Landers." It was like soft-spoken profanity the way it came from his lips.

"Did you—did you find the girl?"

"Pat Cady?"

"Is that her name? I didn't know it."

"She's just a kid," Tracker said, "but she has a lot of spunk." He told Jean about finding Pat, of the fight, and their ride to Jess Hamilton's ranch; how Pat refused to stay there because Hamilton wouldn't lend assistance. "I sent her into town to stay with Pete Randle until this is over."

"I think I would have remained with you," Jean said softly. "It's terrible to be alone, but worse when you've a feeling you must leave the one friend you have."

He smiled at her, secretly glad she felt as she did. "It took some doing. I had to threaten to spank her."

She laughed and it was the first time he'd heard anything like happiness come from her. It gave him an odd yet joyous feeling.

He crossed the room and squatted beside her. "They'll be bringing food soon?"

She nodded, her eyes expectant. "They've fed me regularly. You have a plan, Sam?"

He shook his head. "No. But I've got to watch for an opportunity. I can't understand why they're keeping me alive, anyway."

Almost timidly, she said, "I think I know why."

"How's that?"

"I told them you were an investigator for the Army. I told them if they killed you the whole Army would be on their necks."

He laughed. "True told someone out at the remount station the same thing." He looked at her with suddenly sharp eyes. "Do you know Major O'Donnel?"

"I've met him several times."

"Would you say he knows of what goes on at his post?"

She shook her head. "Major O'Donnel is a fine man, Sam, but very, very much out of place here. He'd be more at home at some old, established Army post in the East. He is miserable here and he won't be happy until he retires. That's my impression of him."

"I read a message there," Tracker said. "The major doesn't know what's going on?"

She nodded, holding him with a glance as sharp as his own. "He leaves everything to Sergeant Winslow."

Tracker was more aware of her than ever, of her quiet beauty and dignity. There was something exciting about her. He'd felt it the first time he met her and each subsequent meeting added to that impression. *She's a thoroughbred,* he thought, *all the way through.*

He bent toward her, not by intention, but as though his movements were directed by a force outside himself. His arms reached out, touching her arms, then dropped to his side. "I'd like to tell you something," he blurted, "when we're out of this. I don't want to say it now . . ."

"Any time is the right time," she whispered.

He looked at her again, and there was a wild singing in his blood, a thump to his heart and as their eyes met something shocking seemed to pass between them. And then, without really knowing how it happened, she was in his arms and their lips were together. He pulled her to him with hungry strength. All his tight restraint fled and the softness of her mouth set fire to his entire being. He felt her arms on his neck and she held him close, with an abandon that surprised him.

When he felt her body tighten he let his arms fall.

"Jean, Jean," he said huskily. "I . . ."

She touched his face with her hand and rose and walked to the window and stood looking through the narrow aperture. He could see the red flush of embarrassment on her lovely face.

He sat there, thinking hard thoughts, trying to push back the memory of her arms on his neck. There was only one way to do that, he realized, and it was direct action.

He surveyed the room. Nothing in it but a chair, a table and the pad on the dirt floor. The walls were a foot thick. There was one narrow slit of a window that neither he or Jean could squeeze through.

If he could make a dummy—he sat back and pulled off his boots. He placed them at the end of the pad. He put his hat at the other end. He removed his shirt, glancing up at Jean as she watched him wide-eyed, and arranged it so it appeared an elbow was projecting over the edge of the pad. Then he took the blanket and carefully covered it. He stood up. A single hasty glance gave the illusion that a man lay under the blanket.

"Jean," he said softly.

She came close to him.

"Go to the door," he whispered. "Tell the guard that I'm dead. Make it convincing, Jean."

"Oh, no, no," she breathed. "It's too dangerous."

"It's just a matter of time," he said grimly, "until they figure out a way to kill me and make it look like an accident. It's a long chance, but we've got to take it."

"But there are others," she protested.

He shook his head in savage impatience. "James and Landers aren't here or they'd be in to gloat. I figure there's just two men here, right now. The longer we wait the more chance others will show." He looked at her. "We've nothing to lose by trying."

"Nothing but our lives," she said. Then suddenly she put her arm out and touched his hand, smiling. "All right, Sam. When you're ready."

He stationed himself beside the door, pressing against the wall and nodded to her.

She walked with a firm step to the door and opened it. "Please," she said, in a choking voice that brought a flush of admiration to Tracker, "this man is dead. He just died! Please take him out!"

CHAPTER 16

Tracker heard the guard's chair grate on the dirt floor and footsteps approached the door. The barrel of the rifle appeared in the doorway and edged further in. Tracker moved with the swiftness of a mountain cat. He grabbed the rifle and yanked hard, pulling the man inside the room, then jerking the rifle from his hands. He raised the rifle and brought it down hard. The guard toppled to the floor. He grunted and struggled to his knees and Tracker slammed the rifle butt down with a solid crack and the man dropped flat on the floor.

Tracker glanced at Jean. She was whitefaced and shaking but he saw she wasn't going to pieces. "Good girl," he said with his lips, and stooped to pull the guard away from the door. He closed the door swiftly, and crossed to the unconscious guard. He bent and unbuckled the gunbelt and, straightening, strapped it around his waist. He sat down and pulled on his boots and slipped on his shirt and buttoned it with swift, sure movements. He tore strips from the blanket and tied the guard and gagged him. He said, in a satisfied whisper, "That was all right. If we can make it as well the rest of the way."

He crossed the room and opened the door again, carrying the rifle. He saw the patio was empty.

There was no sound but that of the wind rustling the tree leaves in the middle of the patio; that and the gurgle of water from the spring.

Tracker stepped through the door, turning his head quickly, motioning for Jean to follow. She followed him closely.

Together, they crossed the patio toward the only exit. Two fast shots split the quiet, the harsh sound exploding inside the patio walls. Tracker dropped, pulling Jean with him. Another shot came, spraying dust into his face. He pushed the rifle ahead of him, cocking it and firing it like a pistol with one hand. A man tumbled out from the hacienda and lay still.

A shot came from the exit. A man fired and then drew quickly back out of sight. *The outside guard,* Tracker thought. No other shots came from the hacienda.

They were screened from the house with the rocks around the spring, but vulnerable to the shooter at the exit. Tracker rose, crouching low, and began a slow walk toward the exit, pumping the lever of the Winchester, directing a stream of bullets into the adobe wall and the corner of the house. He emptied the rifle and dropped it, running forward with the pistol cocked. A man stepped out with his gun aimed at Tracker but Tracker's bullet caught him, knocked him backward against the wall where he slid slowly to the ground. His dying reflexes triggered the pistol and the bullet spat sand between his feet. There was a blue-rimmed hole above his left eye.

Jean came running. She clutched his arm. "You're all right?" she cried.

"Sure, fine." He looked toward the house. "Just three here. That must be all of them. Let's get out of here."

They walked in the hot sun toward the corral. Tracker roped the Rafter H horse and then caught up a piebald for Jean. He saddled the animals and they mounted and turned toward Mule Creek.

The horses went down Mule Creek's main street at a walk. Tracker saw a freight wagon entering town from the east. A single, hip-shot pony stood at the Bird Cage hitching rail. Somewhere in the distance a blacksmith's hammer beat a brassy clangor on an anvil. A gaunt dog lay in the shade of the town pump. Tracker brought his horse into the rail in front of Randle's barber shop. Saddle leather creaked as he stepped down.

He reached his arms and lifted Jean from her horse and stood her on the ground. Pete Randle came from his shop rubbing his face with both hands. He dropped his hands when Tracker spoke.

"Lordy mercy," Randle said and stepped across the walk and into the dust and wrung Tracker's hand while he looked at Jean Rainey. "You all right, miss?"

She smiled. "Fine."

"Come in outta th' sun," Pete said, turning back into his shop.

"Where's Pat?"

Pete grinned. "In th' back, busy as a bumblebee in a chicken coop. Reckon everythin's shinin' like it never shined befo'."

"I'd like Jean to stay here for a while."

"Sho' 'nuff. She'll be mighty welcome. Miss Pat's gonna like havin' somebody to keep her company."

They went through the shop and into the living quarters. Pat dropped the broom she was using and said, "Oh, Sam," and ran to him and hugged him. She saw Jean then, and stepped back, blushing.

"Jean, this is Pat Cady. Pat, Jean Rainey."

The girl and the woman stared at each other. Jean smiled and said, "So nice to meet you, Pat."

"Yes'm," Pat mumbled. "Me too."

"I'd like to wash up," Tracker said, "and get something to eat."

"Sam," Pat said. "Your head—that bloody bandage."

"I got a pretty hard head," Tracker said, laughing.

"You sure you all right?" she insisted.

"One of Leo's pistolmen laid my scalp open," Tracker said. "I'll get over it."

"You come on in the shop," Pete urged. "I'll shave you while the missies get somethin' fo' you to eat." He went out and Tracker followed.

Tracker enjoyed the shave. He relaxed in the chair, while Pete gave him the full treatment, hot towels and plenty of lather. He listened to Pete chatter about the happenings in town. The latest was Arnie True's death in his office. "He'd been stabbed in the back," Pete finished. "Nobody knows who done it and that po' excuse for a sheriff, Shag Wiltse, ain't lookin' very hard."

"Sheriff Hilton coming out of it?"

"He got hit in the lung," Pete explained. "Doc say he some better, but still not out o' danger."

"I suppose by now everybody knows I didn't shoot him," Tracker said.

"Well, ain't nobody talked to Sheriff Hilton. He's been feverish and outta his head most o' the time. Guess nobody'd believe anything he said right now, nohow." He stripped the apron off Tracker. "There, that does it."

Tracker went back into Randle's living quarters. Food was on the table.

"Not much," apologized Pete, "jus' beans, biscuits and salt pork. But maybe it'll hold you."

While they ate, Tracker told Pete something of his plans. "That saddle Pat used, it's an Army saddle. I'm going to take it out to the remount station and ask the major who owns it—or which of his men is missing a saddle. I think maybe if he's not mixed up in this thievery he'll help me find out who is.

"Then again, he might be right up to his ears in

the deal. Anyway, I think I should ask him about it."

"What about your horses? You gonna get your horses back?" Pete asked.

"That's another reason for going out there. See if the Army has bought any of my horses."

"Seems like you ain't had time to do your own work," Pete said. He glanced quickly at the girls and added quickly, "Ain't nothin' more important than you two ladies, believe me. But Mr. Tracker . . ."

"I'll get around to my business sooner or later," Tracker said, grinning at Pete who was flustered at his own thoughtless remarks.

"Maybe we'd better go with you," Pat said defiantly. "We could be some help." She looked at Jean with a scornful challenge in her eyes.

"I'd sure like to have you," Tracker said, "but this time I'd feel better if you'd stay with Pete."

"You reckon you might need me?" Randle asked.

Tracker shook his head. "This is my fight, Pete. You've helped me more than you've any reason to."

"We is both from ole Missy," Pete said, as if that could account for everything. "Reckon us rebs gotta hang together."

"You get me that Army saddle," Tracker said. "That, and taking care of the women folks is a pretty big job."

He didn't attempt to conceal his worry. "Jean and I rode in, right in broad daylight. Sooner or later Leo and Wiltse will get the word. I'm depending on you to stand them off if they show up."

"I'll do it," declared Randle. "I'll shut up the shop and bolt the back door and anybody tries to get through either way will get a load o' buckshot."

Jean poured coffee into Tracker's empty cup. Pete Randle held up his hand when she started to give him more coffee. "I'll have that saddle here by the time you finish," he said, rising, and went out through the back door.

Pat sat with her hands clasped, looking from Jean to Tracker, with a jealousy she couldn't conceal. She knew that her feelings were transparent and that made her all the more miserable.

Tracker went outside to wait for Pete. He could hear the murmur of Jean and Pat talking inside. He shook his head. Pat had looked at him a time or two since he'd got there and she had tears in her eyes. He couldn't figure that out. Maybe it was because she was so young. The loss of her father could have something to do with it. Anyway, it was nice that she'd have Jean Rainey with her, for even a short period. And it looked as though it would be short.

Pete Randle interrupted his thoughts as he

tramped up with the saddle on his shoulder. He dropped it on the ground and scratched his chin. "Sam, I saw Shag Wiltse a few minutes ago. He just come out o' the Chinaman's, standin' there pickin' his teeth. Reckon he don't know you're in town—not yet."

"Then I better get on my way," Tracker said. "I don't want to tangle with him for a while."

He didn't go back into Randle's. He lifted the saddle to his shoulder and walked down the narrow alley to the main street. He looked up and down the street and didn't see anyone. He walked over to the Rafter H horse and started to mount. The Army saddle saved his life, the bullet smacking into it and staggering him. He dropped the saddle and pulled his Colt and turned, all in the same motion, and fired. He missed Shag Wiltse, standing in the door of the Chinaman's. Holding the smoking Colt, Tracker sprinted for the alley. At the same moment Leo James stepped from the Bird Cage with a double-barreled shotgun held hip level and pulled the right-hand trigger. The charge whistled past Tracker's back as he slid into the alley on his belly. The frame wall of Randle's barber shop took the blast hip high, and a round hole appeared in the weathered wood. Tracker got to his feet and faced the street.

James threw down the shotgun and jumped back inside the Bird Cage. The pony at the hitch rack pulled loose and trotted down the street holding its head high to keep the broken reins from dragging. A second later, Leo James and Kirby Landers appeared in the doorway, both of them gray-faced and both of them carrying their pistols.

The echo of the shotgun was still in the street when Wiltse broke the front window of the Chinaman's and shoved out his gun hand. Tracker's bullet seemed to pull him through the broken window. He fell, half in and half out of the Chinaman's, his blood dripping on the wooden floor.

Tracker waited in the alley. He could see neither James nor Landers. Maybe one of them was circling around to come through the alley at the back. He turned and ran as hard as he could toward the back of the alley. He rounded the corner and saw Kirby sneaking toward him and he yelled, "Drop it!"

Kirby swung his gun at him and Sam Tracker dropped flat on his belly and triggered a shot and Kirby dropped his gun and stepped back a pace as if trying to go back the way he'd come; then slowly he sat down and dropped his head between his knees.

Tracker scrambled to his feet and ran back down the alley, toward the main street. Leo James entered the alley when Tracker neared the end. He threw down his pistol and held up his hands, shouting, "Don't shoot an unarmed man, don't shoot!"

Jess Hamilton's crew swept in from one end of town and a detachment of Army entered Mule Creek from the other. They met in the middle of the town and for a moment there was a wild melee, until identification was made. Tracker looked up to see Jean Rainey run out of the shop and toward him. He caught her in his arms and she held herself tight to him. He looked beyond Jean and saw Pat stop, look at him, then turn away.

"I can understand Jess coming to help," Tracker said. "But the Army. How'd they know?"

"I wrote them," Jean said. "I mailed a letter for you to your banker—and to the Army at Coyotero."

"But I thought True caught you writing a letter . . ."

"He did, but that was the one to the Territorial governor. That's the one that didn't get mailed."

Tracker laughed aloud and Jean laughed with him.

Kirby Landers had Tracker's money in a canvas money belt. Jess Hamilton, appointed acting sheriff, returned it to Tracker. This was after he and Tracker and the Army detachment had made a trip to the remount station, where Sergeant Winslow was placed under arrest. Jess had agreed to take Pat Cady to the Rafter H, until her relatives back East could be contacted.

He was embarrassed when he said, "She'll be company for Christine, Sam."

"All I want to do is get back to my ranch," Tracker said.

"I'll take care o' your horse herd," Hamilton promised gruffly, still trying to make amends for turning his back on Tracker for so long. "The Army is wild for them hosses, Sam. And that Arizona Ranger captain says he'd like 'em for his outfit, too."

Sam Tracker took the reins of the two horses and walked down the street to the barber shop and Jean Rainey came out to meet him. Tracker helped her into the saddle. "Your clothes," he said. "What about your clothes?"

She shook her head. "There isn't anything here I want to take with me," she said.

Pat Cady and Pete Randle came out of the shop and stood there, waiting for them to leave. As Tracker and Jean moved out, the two of them called farewells and waved.

On the edge of town, Tracker stopped. "Last chance," he said. "You still want to go with me?"

She leaned toward him and put both arms around his neck. She pulled his head down.

He found her lips warm and alive.

She pulled away. "Yes," she said.

William E. Vance was the author of radio plays, articles, and, beginning in 1952 with *The Branded Lawman* published by Ace Books, of some twenty Western novels. Living for much of his life in Seattle, Washington, in the 1960s he began writing hardcover Western novels, most notably *Outlaw Brand* (Avalon, 1964) and *Tracker* (Avalon, 1964), as well as *Son of a Desperado* for Ace Books in 1966, one of his most notable works. There followed a decade in which he published no Western fiction, only to return, publishing what remain his most outstanding novels with Doubleday: *Drifter's Gold* (1979), *Death Stalks the Cheyenne Trail* (1980), and *Law and Outlaw* (1982), his final novel. "Sound characterization, careful attention to historical background, and a fine story sense were Vance's strong points as a novelist," Bill Pronzini pointed out in *Twentieth-Century Western Writers* (St. James Press, 1991). "Vance's untimely death cut short a promising career which seemed to improve with every book, and his works are well worth reading by anyone interested in the traditional Western story."

Center Point Publishing
600 Brooks Road ● PO Box 1
Thorndike ME 04986-0001 USA

(207) 568-3717

US & Canada:
1 800 929-9108
www.centerpointlargeprint.com